Holiday Grief

JANE BLYTHE

Acknowledgments

I'd like to thank everyone who played a part in bringing this story to life. Particularly my mom who is always there to share her thoughts and opinions with me. My wonderful cover designer Amy who did an amazing job with this stunning cover. My fabulous editor Lisa for all the hard work she puts into polishing my work. My awesome team, Sophie, Robyn, and Clayr, without your help I'd never be able to run my street team. And my fantastic street team members who help share my books with every share, comment, and like!

And of course a big thank you to all of you, my readers! Without you I wouldn't be living my dreams of sharing the stories in my head with the world!

CHAPTER
One

May 12th
5:55 P.M.

There was something wrong with her head.

It felt like someone was stabbing at it with a red-hot fire poker.

Poke.

Poke.

Poke.

Jasmine Crane's stomach revolted at the searing pain, and when bile burned up through her throat, she was powerless to do anything to stop it from erupting out of her mouth and all over herself.

She thought—*thought*—that she heard someone swear but the sound was so distant she wasn't really sure.

Something was wrong with her hearing.

Her eyesight, too, because all she could see was black.

Was she blind?

Going deaf?

Why did her head hurt?

It was too hard to figure it out, the world wouldn't stop spinning.

No, not spinning.

Moving.

It was moving somehow.

Or she was?

Jasmine was so confused.

Something clunked against the backs of her legs sending a jolt of pain through her. Then her wrist hit something and there was more pain.

Pain everywhere.

Reminding her of ...

Something.

Only she couldn't quite remember what.

All she knew was that pain was something she was well acquainted with. That knowledge was so deeply ingrained in her psyche that she would know it anywhere.

There were more clunks, more bumps, more pain, and then the next thing she knew it felt like she was flying.

Instinct had her bracing for pain even though she didn't know where she was or what was going on. But instead of the hard landing she had been expecting, her landing was soft and fluffy.

It almost felt like ...

A bed?

But she wasn't in bed. Shouldn't be in bed. It was daytime. Right?

Confusion swirled along with the dizziness in her head, and she felt sick again.

Turning her head, she emptied the meager contents of her stomach, and there was a howl she swore didn't come from her own lips, and then more pain exploded in her cheek.

Things still didn't make sense, but she did seem to have the where-withal to wonder how she knew the contents of her stomach would be meager.

Because ...

She hadn't eaten much today?

She'd been nervous about the interview?

What interview?

The answer hovered just outside the edges of her mind.

Jasmine tried her best to reach for it and ... a hint of a memory filtered into her mind.

Red.

Red?

Christmas?

Santa?

Those three things went together.

Didn't they?

But why was she thinking about Santa when there was a ... person ... on top of her?

Was she dying?

Was that why she felt so awful?

Maybe the person was going to do CPR?

Only their hands weren't on her chest, positioned above her heart, they were ... on the waistband of her jeans, unzipping them and yanking them down over her hips.

Like a flip had been switched the world suddenly snapped back into focus.

She wasn't blind and she wasn't going deaf, her eyes had simply been closed. Her head hurt so badly because she'd been hit in the head by the man she was interviewing to play the new Santa Claus at the Christmas farm she owned and ran.

The interview hadn't gone well, and it wasn't just because meeting new people gave her serious anxiety, it was because the man gave her the creeps. No way could she imagine letting him work at the farm she had dedicated so many hours to building. He wasn't fit to be around children, and she'd known the second he walked in the door that she wouldn't hire him.

Still, she'd gone through with the interview, telling herself she'd have a nice big bowl of pasta as a reward for peopleing when she was done.

Only that had never happened.

As she'd been showing him out, he'd grabbed her shoulders and slammed her small frame into the door. Her head had taken the brunt of the impact, and she must have passed out. Likely she had a concussion, and with her out of commission, he'd brought her up to her bedroom.

Her *bedroom*.

A space that was supposed to be safe.

This was her little hidey-hole from the world, a place she'd made into a little cocoon that she could curl up in on those days when it felt like just functioning was too far beyond her.

Now this vile, despicable man was tearing at her panties, ripping the thin cotton, breaking the only barrier she had protecting her from what was to come.

Her body was uncooperative, but still, Jasmine lifted her heavy limbs and tried to swat at the man to dislodge his much larger frame.

Thanks to the concussion, her movements were clumsy and ineffectual, and she made zero progress in moving him.

Helplessness filled her as the man laughed at her feeble attempts to fight him off and shoved himself inside her.

Tearing pain made it feel like she was being ripped in two and she turned her head to the side so she didn't have to watch.

Instead, she stared out the window, watching as a lazy cloud rolled across the great blue expanse of sky.

She'd moved out here to get away from people and in a way, herself.

She'd needed something she could lose herself in so she didn't have to think about the terrible choices she'd made and the consequences they'd had not just for herself but for others.

If there was a way to undo the past, right the wrongs, untangle the mess, she'd jump all over it.

But there wasn't.

She was doomed to pay for her sins for all eternity.

As her gaze landed on something on her nightstand, she managed a smile. She wouldn't be the only one paying for her sins for all eternity.

Last night she'd gone to bed early, already anxious about the interview the following day. In fact, she'd been so anxious that she'd brought her dinner up to bed with her, needing to be in her safe place.

That decision might well save her life.

Grabbing the knife, she used every bit of strength she had and slammed it into the man's neck.

CHAPTER
Two

May 12th
7:14 P.M.

"Do we know how bad she's hurt?" Detective Adam Abram asked his partner as they drove toward the farm. The call had come in a few minutes ago, and since they happened to be in the area interviewing a suspect in a recent vehicular manslaughter case, they had called in to say they would take the case.

"Just that a woman called in saying she'd been attacked," Jessica Spears replied. A year younger than him, they'd been partners for a couple of years and worked well together.

Both single parents of young children, they connected in a way a lot of people couldn't. Raising a kid was hard, but raising one on your own was one of the toughest things you could ever do. Finding a way to be both mom and dad and juggle all the responsibilities of work, house, and child without a partner to back you up was almost impossible.

Flat out without the support of his family, Adam didn't think he'd be able to do it.

"You been out there?" he asked. Apparently, their victim was the owner of the Christmas Farm just outside of town.

Opening around three years ago, it had become an instant hit. The place was open year-round, but only on the weekends from January through October. After Halloween, it was open every day. There was a full-time Santa who you could visit with. There were reindeer, an elf workshop, orchards, vegetable gardens, horses, and huskies. In the winter you could go on sleigh and sled rides. There was an ice-skating rink, snowman-building contests, and snowball fights. The place was magical even for an adult.

"Oh yeah. Freddie *loves* the place," Jessica replied.

"Claire too," he said. His four-year-old daughter might not remember the mother who had died from cancer when she was only a few months old, but she had definitely inherited her love of all things Christmas.

Adam hoped the quiet woman who ran the farm was okay.

Jasmine Crane. An enigma. A few years younger than his own twenty-seven years, she had blonde hair that hung down past her back-side and huge green eyes that always held a haunted gleam.

No one saw much of her, she rarely left her property, and when she did, she kept her head down and her distance from everyone. Although he knew she worked tirelessly to run the farm, the times he'd taken Claire there he hadn't seen her. She was more of a behind-the-scenes kind of woman.

A few minutes later they were pulling into the driveway of the property.

Since it was a Thursday evening, no one was there, giving the farm a somewhat eerie feeling.

Because it was a Christmas farm there were decorations up all year round, and the brightly colored tinsel and garlands draped around the trees lining the driveway seemed incongruous with the reason for them being there.

Several buildings made up the property. They were all log cabins, highlighted with red and white shutters and doors. Around the back there was a cute little two-story house that he knew was where Jasmine lived.

Parked outside of it was a dark gray SUV.

It didn't belong to Jasmine Crane.

Exchanging a glance with Jessica, he knew his partner was on the same page as he was. Jasmine's assailant was still there. If her attacker was still there, how had she been able to get to a phone to call for help?

Weapons in hand, they climbed out of their car and made their way toward the front door.

It was sitting partially open, and as he got closer, Adam saw blood smeared on the doorframe.

Nodding his head at it, Jessica nodded to say she'd seen it too and they stepped inside the quiet house.

The *too* quiet house.

There wasn't a sign of life.

Had Jasmine's assailant got his hands on her after she made the 911 call?

They cleared a living room on their right, and an office on their left. Next, they cleared a dining room, and a large open kitchen with a couch, entertainment stand, and dining table.

With an empty downstairs they moved to the staircase.

As he got further up, he could hear the soft sound of crying.

Jasmine.

Picking up the pace, Adam moved directly toward the sound and crossed the hall, entering the master bedroom.

The scene that met him was not what he had been expecting.

On the bed lay the body of a man. From the amount of blood soaking the covers, Adam already knew he was dead. Jasmine cowered in the corner, tears streaming down her cheeks, blood streaking one side of her head from a nasty-looking gash on her temple.

It didn't take a genius to figure out what had gone on in this room.

The fact that Jasmine's jeans were unzipped and shoved partway down her legs was just further proof.

When she saw them, panic immediately filled her face, and her gaze locked on their weapons.

"I didn't mean to. I just had to make him stop," she screeched.

Even from across the room, he could see her press against the wall until her trembling body was plastered against it.

Something shifted inside him as he put his gun away, held his hands up, palms out, and very slowly moved toward her. If she thought she was going to be punished for defending herself she couldn't be more wrong.

"It's okay, green eyes," he soothed, "you did good. You did what you had to do."

"Y-you didn't come to take me to j-jail?" she stammered.

When he reached her, he lowered himself cautiously down to crouch before her. He wanted to reach out, touch her, offer comfort, but he was afraid that touching her when she'd just been assaulted would shove her over the edge. Instead, he locked his gaze on hers and infused every ounce of confidence into his voice he could. "You did the right thing," he said firmly.

For a long moment, she studied him and he couldn't figure out what she was looking for. Then she gave a noisy sob and threw herself into his arms, buried her face against his neck, and clung to him.

There was another shift inside him, one he didn't quite understand as he wrapped his arms around her and held her tight against his chest.

CHAPTER
Three

June 1st
3:40 P.M.

The sound of something scraping against glass made Jasmine shriek, and she jumped about a foot in the air.

Since she'd been making a snack, peanut butter on bread, and had the jar and a knife in her hands, both went cluttering to the floor as her fingers curled into fists and automatically sprung up ready to defend herself.

Every single little sound made her jump these days.

It had been a really long couple of weeks.

Despite multiple assurances from the cops and the DA, she still wasn't convinced that she wasn't going to be charged with murder for killing the man she now knew as Rupert Brooks. A known rapist, already out on bail when he'd applied with a fake resume for the job as Santa at her farm, he had also been wanted in the rapes of two other women in the area.

Nobody seemed to care that he was dead.

Nobody but her at least.

And she didn't care in the sense that she was upset he was dead, just that she had been the one to do it, and even though she'd been defending herself there was a part of her that felt she had to be punished for it.

Whenever her phone rang—which given she ran a business was often—or there was a knock at her door—less common but more scary —her heart began to race, her palms grew sweaty, and she prepared to be told she was being arrested.

Just payment for past sins as far as she was concerned.

Another scrape filled her quiet kitchen, and this time she realized it was just a tree brushing against the window.

Nothing to worry about.

No one coming to hurt her.

The kitchen door suddenly banged open, and she screamed as she spun toward it to find Detective Adam Abram standing there, his weapon in his hand.

Even though she'd been expecting it, knowing she was about to be taken into custody had her heart racing.

Still, she deserved it, and Adam had been nice to her so she didn't want to make this harder on him.

Lowering her hands, which were still in fists and up protecting her face, she held them out so he could cuff her.

Adam's dark eyes softened, and he holstered his weapon. "Keep telling you, green eyes, that you're not going to be arrested."

"But I killed someone."

"You killed the man raping you to protect yourself," he corrected. "Now I heard you scream. What's wrong?" His gaze roamed the room as though searching for a threat, and Jasmine felt her cheeks heat.

"Oh, I keep forgetting to trim the branches on the tree by the window, it keeps scratching against the glass and startling me," she admitted. Although she didn't know the man well, he'd been nice to her the night she'd been assaulted, holding her while she cried and riding in the ambulance with her to the hospital. He'd stayed while she'd been examined and endured the rape kit, then arranged for a female officer to stay with her overnight and bring her home the next day. Since then, he'd come by occasionally to check in on her, and he was always so careful to keep his distance while also working to put her at ease and even to make her laugh.

Something she'd actually done despite believing it was impossible after she'd committed the most atrocious of sins.

Adam tutted. "You should have told me, I would have taken care of that for you."

Jasmine frowned at him. "Why would I have told you?" It was something she could easily take care of herself, and even if she couldn't, she had ground maintenance staff she could ask. The only reason she hadn't was because she was avoiding contact with people as much as she possibly could.

"Why wouldn't you?" he retorted. "I put my number in your phone and told you to call if you needed anything."

"I thought you meant if I was like ... in need of a cop." What else would he have meant? Wasn't like they were friends or anything. Barely even acquaintances. He was a nice guy, sure, and he felt sorry for her, she got that, but he had his own life. Why would he care about coming over to cut a branch off a tree for her?

"Well, now you know better." His face broke into a huge grin. "I have something for you."

"What do you mean?"

Adam laughed, a free, joyful sound that stirred up memories of the past, of when she used to be that carefree.

Felt like a lifetime ago.

"What do you think someone means when they say they have something for you?" he teased, coaxing a smile out of her. "Come on."

When he held up his hand to her, she stared at it.

He wanted her to hold his hand?

To touch him?

The thought sent a wave of icy dread washing over her, her entire body rebelling at the thought of physical contact.

But he didn't hurry her.

Didn't push.

Simply stood there with his hand out waiting. Leaving the ball in her court. She could take his hand, or walk past him, and she knew he wouldn't mind, wouldn't make her feel bad or stupid for not being ready for human contact yet.

For some reason, the very fact that he wouldn't force her to do anything she didn't want to do was the thing that had her inching closer. Her hand lifted slowly, trembling as it did so, and with almost excruciating slowness, she placed it in his.

As soon as she did his fingers curled loosely around hers, warm and strong. Instead of making her feel panicky, it filled her with a sense of security she had been so badly lacking for such a very long time.

Tugging her along with him, Adam led her outside to where his truck was parked. Emanating from the vehicle was a yapping sound that reminded her of a puppy.

Jasmine cocked her head and watched with interest as Adam released her hand, opened the back door of the car, and lifted out a crate.

The yapping was much louder, and she could see a tan and brown body wiggling excitedly inside.

"You got a dog?" she asked.

"Nope." Adam opened the crate door and just managed to grab hold of the wriggling bundle of energy. "I got her for you. Her name is Fauna, and she's four months old. She flunked out of her police training course and she needs a home. She's sweet and affectionate, she's potty trained and knows all her basic commands, and her trainer promised that if you want to continue to train her, he'll help. She'll make a good guard dog. She just doesn't like big crowds so she can't do police work. She needs someone to love her and take care of her, and I think ... maybe you need that too."

Truer words had never been spoken.

It had been so long since she'd been loved.

Even longer since she'd had someone to take care of her.

Once upon a time she'd had that, but she'd thrown it away for a man she believed had loved her.

She'd been so very wrong.

Now as she reached out and took the puppy into her arms and was immediately rewarded with a wet kiss to the cheek, Jasmine realized how very much she'd missed it.

CHAPTER
Four

August 24th
10:52 A.M.

This was likely a very bad idea.

Okay, scratch that. There was no likely. It was definitely a bad idea.

Still, he didn't stop.

Didn't turn his car around and head home like he should.

It was like the universe kept drawing him to her.

Adam turned his car into the driveway of the Christmas Farm and headed straight for Jasmine's place.

It was becoming a habit, bordering on an addiction. He just couldn't seem to stay away from the woman.

There was something alluring about her. It wasn't her looks because he'd seen plenty of pretty women in the past, he'd been married to one. It wasn't that he felt sorry for her, although of course, he did feel empathy for the fact that she had been violated in her own home.

To be honest, he wasn't quite sure what it was.

Maybe her vulnerability?

Her loneliness?

Or it was the fact that a light flicked on in her huge green eyes every time she saw him.

Those first few times he'd popped by to see her, make sure she was coping because she didn't seem to have any family there for her, her eyes had been dull. Empty. Lifeless.

Somehow, it had become his mission to change that. At first, he'd just wanted to coax out a smile, then a laugh, then he'd wanted to make her feel safe, and now it had grown into something more.

He was falling for her.

It was crazy. She'd been raped and beaten just three months ago and was in no place to be considering a relationship. Add in the fact that she'd been reclusive even before she was assaulted, and he thought he was probably fighting a losing battle here.

Thing was, it was a battle he wanted to fight. To win.

Just as he was parking outside her place the front door opened and a blur of fur came speeding out.

By the time he was out of the vehicle, Fauna was spinning in excited circles, waiting for the pet and the treat she knew she was going to get.

Crouching down, Adam ruffled the puppy's silky coat then handed over a unicorn toy, squeaking it and making the puppy yip in excitement. What good dog didn't love a squeaky toy? Next, he handed over the dog cookie. It was in the shape of a bone and covered in pink sprinkles. Fauna licked his hand in thanks and then took the cookie, promptly running a few steps away to protect her treat.

"You spoil her rotten," Jasmine said from where she stood in the doorway leaning against the frame. She looked good, more relaxed than he'd seen her since the assault. Her long legs were pale, telling him she still wasn't spending much time outdoors, but the denim shorts and tank top hugged her slender frame telling him that at least she was taking care of herself and eating regular meals.

"No more than you do," he retorted as he picked up the unicorn and carried it toward the door.

"You keep bringing her a new toy every time you come by and I'm going to have to buy her another basket to fit them all in."

"Hey, I'm only responsible for half of the toys." When Jasmine arched a brow he amended, "Three quarters." The arched brow didn't lower. "Eighty percent? Ninety? Ninety-five?"

"At least."

"You've bought her some too."

"Two. She has like thirty toys. I think that means you pretty much gave her ninety-five percent of all her toys."

"Math nerd," he muttered teasingly.

Jasmine swatted at his shoulder as he brushed past her and into her house. It wasn't the first time she had initiated contact and as it did every other time his heart did this weird little stutter in his chest.

Falling for Jasmine was so incredibly stupid and yet he couldn't stop himself even if he wanted to, and he definitely didn't want to.

"Just because I liked math doesn't make me a nerd," she told him as she whistled for Fauna, who came trotting up the porch steps and into the house.

"Sure it doesn't."

His goading made her huff and he laughed. Seeing her begin to relax, especially in his company, made all the drives out here to her farm more than worth it. In the last few months, those visits had become more frequent, and now he was out here at least a couple of times a week.

"You're impossible," she huffed, making him laugh all over again.

"Tell me which sink needs fixing, Jas," he said as he nudged her out of the way and closed the front door. When she'd called last night to tell him that one of her sinks was backing up and overflowing and asked if maybe he could come and help, he'd about jumped up and down cheering.

Finally.

He'd earned her trust enough that she was now comfortable asking him for help. He knew she had maintenance staff who could fix this for her, but he also knew while she'd ask them to do something on the property letting anyone into her home was hard for her.

"Kitchen," she replied as the three of them headed for the kitchen, Fauna bouncing on ahead. The now six-month-old puppy had been working hard on her training as had Jasmine, and she was well on her way to becoming a well-trained guard dog.

In the kitchen, he headed straight for the sink while Fauna trotted over to her bed and resumed chewing on a toy wand, and Jasmine stood in the middle of the room wringing her hands nervously.

If there was one thing he'd learned it was not to push her. When she was ready, she'd admit whatever was going on with her. For now, he just got to work on fixing her sink.

"Umm, I was thinking, since you're here, and it'll take you a bit to fix the sink, and it's getting close to lunchtime, maybe you want me to fix you something to eat before you go?" Jasmine finally asked.

Since his back was to her, Jasmine didn't see his grin or the relief he felt.

He was making progress.

Patience.

All he had to do was be patient, continue earning Jasmine's trust, and then when she was ready he'd ask her out on a date.

Although this felt kind of like a date and he knew from the anxious waves flowing off her Jasmine felt the same way.

"I'd love to stay and have lunch with you."

CHAPTER
Five

December 19th
11:03 A.M.

It was totally crazy given that she owned and ran a Christmas farm which was of course geared for kids and families, but children made Jasmine nervous.

No, nervous wasn't a strong enough word.

They totally freaked her out.

It wasn't that she disliked them, quite the opposite in fact. She found kids to be intelligent, empathetic, curious, and full of life and energy. She liked them a whole lot but being around them stirred up memories she'd rather forget.

Memories it was getting harder and harder to keep buried.

All because of the man she was going to see.

Adam had been a constant in her life these last seven months. Honestly, she didn't know what she would have done without him. Bit by bit he had earned her trust with his patience and steadfastness. Their relationship had long since moved from cop and victim of crime to friendship. And now ...

Now it felt like more.

Felt like too much.

That might not be as terrifying as it was if he didn't have a daughter. A sweet, adorable little four-year-old named Claire.

Claire who was sweet, sassy, and bubbly and for some completely unknown reason had become immediately taken with Jasmine the moment they met. It had happened by accident about two months ago. After putting off hiring a new Santa for her farm because she couldn't handle doing it after what happened last time, she'd reached the deadline. If she didn't hire someone, she'd miss the entire Christmas season, and that meant she might as well give up her farm.

Since she couldn't do that, she'd reached out to Adam who had readily agreed to do the interviews for her. Only when he'd come over his babysitter had fallen through because his mom had come down with the flu, so he'd brought along his daughter.

Because Adam had to conduct the interview, she was left in charge of the little girl. They'd baked and decorated cupcakes. Jasmine had given her a piano lesson when Claire caught sight of it and wanted to play it, and they'd colored. Before leaving, Claire had given her a picture she'd drawn of the two of them baking.

The picture still hung on her fridge.

Jasmine liked the little girl a lot. She was as sweet as her daddy, but being around her stirred up all kinds of past trauma.

Trauma she hadn't dealt with yet.

Running didn't count as dealing.

Neither did hiding.

As her gaze fell on the daddy and daughter duo, she felt a pang in her chest. They could never be hers. Not really. And it had nothing to do with her assault.

Still if life was different, if *she* was different, not such a screwup and disappointment then maybe ...

But life wasn't different, and neither was she. Jasmine knew she would never deserve a love as pure as Adam and Claire would offer.

Almost as if the pair could feel the weight of her gaze they turned as one, smiles lighting their faces when they saw her.

They were too good for her, and she cared about them enough that she should walk away, but she wasn't sure she was strong enough to actually do it.

Not when they beamed joy into her life instead of judgment.

Flickering her fingers in greeting, Jasmine tried not to shrink away from the crowd of people in the pottery barn as she walked toward them. Pottery was just one of the many special activities she offered at this time of year. It should make her happy to see the business she had worked hard to build doing so well, but she hadn't done well with crowds in a while, and even less since her assault in May.

"Jazzy!" Claire squealed, bouncing off the stool she'd been sitting on to engulf her in a huge hug.

"Careful, pumpkin, you're getting clay and paint all over Jasmine," Adam said, reaching to extricate his daughter from her hold.

"It's okay, Claire," Jasmine said quickly, not wanting the little girl to get in trouble even as she knew Adam was a fair and reasonable parent. "I always wear old clothes when hanging on the farm because this is a place where we have fun and don't have to worry about being clean."

"Guess what I'm making," Claire demanded, bouncing in Jasmine's arms.

Casting a glance at the black lump of pottery sitting on the table, she didn't want to admit she had no idea what it was supposed to be, so she quickly looked over at Adam. He stifled a laugh and held up his hands mimicking playing a piano, and she gave a discreet nod.

"Umm ..." Jasmine tipped her head to the side as though thoughtfully studying the little girl's creation. "Well ... it looks like a ... piano?"

"It is!" Claire squealed delightedly. Her pure joy and excitement over the holiday season was infectious, and Jasmine's smile became less brittle and more genuine. "Guess who it's for."

"Your daddy?"

"Nope. I made daddy ... oops," Claire looked over her shoulder at her father, "it's 'posed to be a surprise."

"Then keep that big mouth of yours closed," Adam teased, tickling the backs of Claire's knees and making her giggle.

"Your grandma? Grandpa?" Claire shook her head no to both. "Aunts? Uncles? One of your cousins? A friend from school?" More nos. "I give up. Who did you make it for?"

"It's for you, silly," Claire informed her.

Emotion clogged her throat.

It had been a *long* time since she received a Christmas gift. While she had reconnected with her family a little before she started the farm, things were different between them than when she was a child. There was a distance there, one she didn't know how to bridge.

"For me?" she whispered.

"Cos you likes playin' piano, and you's real good. I want to learn to play songs like you do. Daddy said you could teach me if you have time."

Claire's hopeful brown eyes looked at her expectantly, even as Adam stood and winced.

"Sorry, I was going to ask you about it," he explained. "She's been insisting she wants to learn to play as well as you."

In this moment, she would give this special little girl anything she wanted. This sweet child was healing some of Jasmine's old wounds, and she didn't even know it.

CHAPTER
Six

February 8th
7:47 P.M.

He was early, but he couldn't wait any longer.

Finally.

His patience had won out, and Jasmine had agreed to go on a date with him.

Adam couldn't wipe the grin off his face as he gathered the bouquet of flowers he'd picked up on the way here, along with the picnic basket he'd packed, and climbed out of his truck. Since Jasmine was more than a little wary about leaving her property, he thought they'd do something here for their first official date.

Even before he got to the front door, he could hear Fauna yapping excitedly. Getting that puppy for her, a spur-of-the-moment decision when his friend was talking about the little German Shepard who flunked out of his class, had turned out to be one of the best he'd ever made. The puppy was devoted to Jasmine and had taken a real shine to

Claire as well, which was perfect because if he played his cards right the four of them might be a family one day.

It might be crazy to think that far into the future when he and Jasmine were only just about to have their first date, but if he wasn't seriously interested, he wouldn't have been building a foundation these last nine months.

Besides, when he'd met his wife, he'd known from that very first moment that they were going to wind up together. Why should things be any different this time around?

Knocking on her front door, it took barely fifteen seconds for her to answer, and when she did his jaw dropped open in shock.

Usually, Jasmine dressed for comfort: jeans and a sweater if it was cold, jean shorts and a tank top or T-shirt if it was hot, but today she looked like she'd just stepped off the cover of a fashion magazine. Instead of in a ponytail like usual, her long hair hung down her back in a mass of golden waves. She'd added a little mascara and eyeshadow making her green eyes practically glow like emeralds. Her charcoal gray dress hugged her slender body, and the knee-high black boots emphasized her long, lean legs.

Perfection.

"Umm, hi," Jasmine said, and he realized he'd been staring.

"You look gorgeous," he told her, then held out the bouquet. "These are for you. And this," he bent down and held out a bone to Fauna, "is for you."

Fauna took the bone and gave him a tail wag as she trotted off to eat it.

"Thanks for the flowers, they're beautiful," Jasmine said.

"You're beautiful."

She blushed adorably, and her hands self-consciously smoothed at the skirt of her dress. "I wasn't sure what to wear because you didn't tell me where we were going."

"We're not going far."

"Should I change then?"

"Don't you dare. But you will need your coat," he added.

After quickly putting the flowers in a vase and kissing Fauna goodbye, she met him by the door. When he held out her coat for her, she slipped her arms through the sleeves, and when his hands trailed down her arms, and he clasped one of hers she didn't pull away.

Adam loved it when she let him touch her.

He knew exactly what level of trust he had earned when she allowed him to put a hand anywhere on her body. They hadn't known each other before her assault so he had no past to count on, everything he'd worked hard to earn from her had been work. Enjoyable, but he'd known he had to take his time, be patient, always keep in mind what she'd been through, and make sure not to push her too hard and freak her out.

Now she was allowing him to take her on a date and hold her hand. One day, when she allowed him the privilege of kissing her, he'd be over the moon.

Baby steps though.

That's what he reminded himself as they walked outside into the crisp evening. Spring might still be officially over a month away but the weather the last few days had been pleasant. Didn't mean there wouldn't be more snow coming, but for now, it was nice to enjoy the milder weather.

They made it all the way to the bottom of the porch steps when Jasmine suddenly froze.

Panic filled her huge green eyes as she looked up at him, but since she didn't try to tug her hand free he didn't release her.

Instead, he just stood there. Waiting. Giving her time to work through whatever fears she was battling.

"I don't ... I'm not ... I don't know if I can do this," Jasmine said. There was a pleading quality to her voice that told him what she needed was reassurance.

"The ball's in your court, green eyes. If you aren't ready, I understand. We can go back to just hanging out together. There's no time frame for healing. You'll be ready when you're ready."

"What if I'm never ready? What if I don't deserve to be happy?"

And there it was.

The truth in those whispered words hit him hard.

Adam didn't need to know this went deeper than what had happened last May. It was why she shut herself up here on her farm, interacted with people as little as possible, had no friends, and a strained relationship with her family.

Lifting the hand he still held, Adam touched a kiss to it. "Whatever sins you think you committed are you truly sorry for them?"

"Yes, yes, so much yes."

"Have you tried to make amends for those sins?"

"The best way I know how."

"Would you commit those same sins again?"

"No. Never. Not ever." The desperation in her voice spoke of the guilt she heaped on her shoulders, but he couldn't imagine what sins Jasmine believed she could have committed.

"Then you deserve to be happy." As much as he wanted to add that he wanted to be the one to make her happy he didn't. Because Jasmine had to want it for herself.

He would fight for her, but believing she deserved happiness and a future was a battle Jasmine would have to wage on her own.

Adam just prayed she was victorious because he was already in deep.

CHAPTER
Seven

February 8th
9:39 P.M.

"Another one?"

Jasmine rubbed her stomach. They'd been eating hot dogs cooked in the fire Adam had built for over an hour. Usually, she didn't even particularly like hot dogs, didn't dislike them they just weren't a favorite, but cooked over an open fire like this ... they were the most delicious thing she'd ever eaten.

Or maybe it was the company that made them so yummy.

"Well ... I probably shouldn't," she said. Watching her figure wasn't something she usually cared about. After all, who would she be trying to impress? Working out was different, especially after her attack, that was about keeping her body toned and as strong as it could be.

"Oh, you totally should," Adam countered, grabbing another hot dog and sticking it on the long metal tongs they'd been using to cook them.

"You're trying to fatten me up aren't you," she teased, but didn't tell him no as he moved the hot dog into the flames. After talking her off a ledge, they'd hiked a little way into the woods to a small clearing. There he had set up a campfire and a couple of Adirondack chairs. He'd lit the fire once they got there and regaled her with stories of camping trips he'd taken with his family when he was a kid. He'd been a cheeky little boy, always getting into mischief, and it made her think of the things she'd missed out on as a kid.

Her family hadn't been picture-perfect like Adam's.

Far from it.

Certainly not the worst. There was no abuse, alcoholism, or drug use, but they'd barely made ends meet after her dad walked out on them when she was four. With seven little mouths to feed, her mom had no time for anything other than work, and while Jasmine was the third youngest, with three older brothers and an older sister and younger twin sisters, she still had to pull her weight.

There was no time or money even for things such as camping. There was barely enough for food and second-hand clothes.

But that was a long time ago, and she was doing pretty well these days thanks to a benefactor who had loaned her the money to start up her Christmas farm. Those days seemed like a dozen lifetimes ago, and thanks to Adam, she was actually finding joy in life.

A terrifying thing to a person who had escaped hell.

Happiness could be ripped away in a heartbeat.

That she knew all too well.

"Not with the hot dogs, but maybe with dessert," Adam joked back, winking as he nodded at the bag of marshmallows, chocolate bars, and crackers.

"Ooh, s'mores!" It had been a long time since she'd had any. Not since one night when she was ten. Alone with her little sisters, they'd made s'mores over the gas stove. It was dangerous looking back on it but a whole lot of fun.

"Got to have dessert. Want more juice?" he asked.

Along with the hot dogs and s'mores, he'd packed a thermos of hot juice, the perfect drink to go along with their meal.

"Mmm, yeah, I do." While she got up to pour herself another cup of juice, Adam pulled the hot dog out of the fire and sat down in his seat.

When she went to move past him to her chair, Adam put an arm around her waist and tugged her into his lap.

For a moment Jasmine froze.

Panic bubbled inside her.

This was the closest she'd been to a man since her assault, and even before then none of her male interactions had been positive.

Jasmine had believed there was no such thing as a good man.

Men were selfish and cruel. They took without offering anything in return. They hurt, ridiculed, and in the end, they walked away leaving you broken.

But not Adam.

Adam was everything she thought didn't exist.

Proof that the fairytales she'd loved as a child occasionally came true.

Only she wasn't sure whether the two of them could ever have that happy ever after ending because despite his words earlier she wasn't sure she was deserving of happiness.

Still, she trusted this man, liked him, perhaps was even falling in love with him. His reliability, patience, and willingness to prove himself to her even though he personally had never done anything to hurt her.

So she didn't move.

Instead, she forced her muscles to relax one by one. Starting at her feet, she worked her way up her body until she could relax into his hold.

The moment she did, Adam moved a hand resting it on her hip anchoring her against him.

That action, tiny as it might be, insignificant even to most, made a swell of emotion flood her chest. He was there, he wasn't going anywhere. For nine long months he had proven that to her over and over again.

Happy endings might not exist, or maybe they did.

Perhaps she deserved one, or her past sins had already condemned her.

Jasmine didn't know, and for now, she wanted to set aside her brain and just feel, let her heart guide her.

Once upon a time she'd tried that, it had failed in spectacular fashion, but she was older now, and definitely wiser. This time she was sure she wasn't making a mistake, and if she was, at least she wasn't putting anyone, not even herself, in any physical danger.

Slowly, she lifted an arm and draped it around Adam's shoulders, allowing him to snuggle her closer.

One of his hands cupped her cheek, his touch almost impossibly gentle as his fingertips feathered across her forehead and then her temple.

Their gazes met and something seemed to flow between them, an energy she didn't quite understand.

But she felt it.

It flowed through her, empowering her, mesmerizing her almost.

Her head dipped, Adam's tilted up, but he didn't push her. Like he always did, he made sure that she knew the ball was firmly in her court.

That power was enough to have her lean in and press her lips to his.

As soon as she did, he took control of the kiss, his hands framed her face, his tongue swept into her mouth, and for the first time since she was a little girl, Jasmine really did believe that happy endings might be possible.

CHAPTER
Eight

September 30th
1:28 P.M.

So, she was a little late, that was okay, so long as she turned up.

Adam would put up with anything from Jasmine. He knew that she was struggling and working hard to overcome her issues, but the one thing he couldn't allow was his daughter being hurt.

Claire was his world, had been from the moment they found out Meredith was pregnant. There wasn't anything he wouldn't do for her, and the only thing that could make him stop fighting for what he knew he and Jasmine could have was if she hurt his daughter.

Turning five was a big deal, and Claire had been excited to invite Jasmine. Even though he knew she struggled in groups of people she had agreed immediately. Over the last three weeks, he kept expecting to get a call or text from her telling him she couldn't make it. Each time he picked her up to take her out on a date—sometimes just the two of them, other times they did things together with Claire—he was waiting for her to inform him she couldn't do it.

But she never did.

He'd placed an enormous amount of trust in her. Jasmine might think he was the only one contributing to their slowly blooming relationship, but she would be wrong. She had her issues, yes, but he had a daughter he didn't trust just anyone to be part of her life.

Jasmine had what it took to be an amazing stepmom, and one day an amazing mom to their kids, but she had to believe it.

"Daddy, is Jassy coming soon?" Claire asked, appearing at his side.

In addition to their family, there were a dozen little girls from Claire's school here as well. They had a bouncy castle, miniature golf, and even though the weather had started cooling down the kids had wanted to play in the pool. More than enough to keep a little girl happy and occupied, but his daughter kept coming to ask him if Jasmine was going to be here soon.

"Soon, honey," he said, praying Jasmine wasn't making him lie.

"What if she doesn't come?" There was concern in his daughter's eyes that he didn't like seeing there. She had taken to Jasmine immediately, and their relationship was growing alongside his and Jasmine's.

Come on, green eyes. Don't let me down.

As though his words conjured her out of thin air, Claire squealed and darted off toward the gate where Jasmine was standing, hovering nervously.

Adam grinned. He never should have doubted Jasmine. Even though she had issues, secrets she hadn't shared with him yet, she loved his little girl, he knew she did, and she was no coward. She'd fought for her life and killed her rapist. She wasn't going to let a fear of crowds stop her from putting a smile on a child's face.

Claire threw herself into Jasmine's arms, and he could see her relax as she hugged the little girl.

"Happy birthday, sweet girl," Jasmine was saying as he reached them.

"I thought you weren't coming," Claire said, no hiding what they were thinking for small children.

"No way I would let my favorite girl down," Jasmine said. There was a little guilt in her eyes that his daughter missed, enough to tell him she'd had to battle against herself to get here. But she *was* here, and that was all that mattered.

Next time he'd have to have more faith in her.

"Is that my present?" Claire asked, eyeing the bright pink box tied with purple ribbon.

Both he and Jasmine laughed, and he felt her relax further, no longer focused on the birthday party guests, but on the reason she was here. How could he not be falling in love with a woman who put his daughter and her needs above her own fears?

"Sure is," Jasmine replied.

"Can I open it now?"

"We were going to do presents after cake," he reminded his daughter.

Claire pouted. "But, Daddy, this is *Jassy's* present. I want to open it now."

"Guess I can't argue with the birthday girl," he said, giving permission.

Jasmine handed over the box, and Claire made quick work undoing the bow. When she lifted off the lid she gasped and reached inside, lifting out a large wooden box. It was carved with an image of a little girl —clearly Claire—and several animals playing around her.

"Open it up," Jasmine said.

When Claire lifted the lid of the wooden box music immediately began to play, and a carousel with the animals carved on the lid began to spin slowly.

"Look, it's me," Claire squealed in delight as she spotted the girl riding on a giraffe. Giraffes were Claire's favorite animal so he knew that was no coincidence.

"It's a music box," Jasmine said.

"That must have cost you a fortune." This wasn't an off-the-shelf music box. She'd had someone make it for her, choosing something she knew Claire would love.

"Claire deserves it." Jasmine jutted out her chin as though daring him to disagree, and how could he? These two women were everything to him.

"It's going to go on my special shelf," Claire said, still staring in awe at the music box.

"High praise," he told Jasmine. "Only her very best things go on that shelf."

"I'm honored." Jasmine's green eyes were soft as she looked down at the little girl. His instincts were spot on when he knew not long after he met her that she would be the mother Claire deserved. A mother who would love his little girl almost as much as Meredith would have.

"Let's go jump on the castle," Claire announced.

"Oh, uh, I'm not usually a fan of that bouncing movement," Jasmine said.

"It's okay, Daddy can hold your hand," Claire told her.

Ruffling Claire's hair he grinned at Jasmine. "Look at my girl playing matchmaker."

Claire's face scrunched in confusion. "What's matchmaker? Do they make matches to light my candles?"

He and Jasmine both laughed, and when he held out one hand to Jasmine and one to Claire, both his girls took them without hesitation. "No, honey. A matchmaker is someone who helps a boy and a girl fall in love."

"Fall in love?" Claire asked. "Are you falling in love with Jassy?"

Jasmine's green eyes looked huge in her face as she stared up at him, awaiting his answer. An answer that was easy to give because it was completely true.

"I sure am."

CHAPTER
Nine

"Oh, Jett. Hi," Jasmine said as she opened her front door to find her brother standing there.

Her oldest brother never missed an opportunity to make sure she knew how disappointed he was in her. Nine years older than her, by the time she'd made her colossal, life-changing mistake he'd already been out of the home and in the FBI. He had no idea what things had been like then. Sure, when he'd been young he had stepped up to help financially support the family, but at least he'd been allowed to have a life if he wanted one.

By the time she was the oldest in the home—Jett gone, her older sister who was six years older than her gone, and the twin brothers who were three years older gone—their mom had forbidden anything but school, a job, and chores. Watching her four oldest kids dedicate themselves to their schoolwork and then college, Mom had decided that she wanted the three younger kids to do the same.

Which meant no boyfriends.

At sixteen, a boyfriend had seemed way more important in her pre-mistake life than in her post-mistake life.

Running away had been stupid, and she couldn't blame it on being young. She had known better, but she'd done it anyway, she just hadn't understood the world was a dark and evil place.

Two years of hell had educated her on that real quick.

"Mom is disappointed you're not coming to Thanksgiving dinner," Jett said without preamble. He was the closest thing she remembered to a father, but he was so disapproving, so judgmental that it was hard to spend time around him. If he'd ever made her feel like something other than a spoiled disappointment, then maybe she would have gone to him when she needed help.

"I never go," she reminded him. At eighteen when she'd finally escaped, she'd made contact with her family at the encouragement of a social worker to let them know she was still alive, but those two years stood between them, a silent, unseen barrier, but a barrier none-theless.

He tutted. "You're twenty-four years old now, Jasmine, not a baby any longer. And we've all heard around town that you've been dating Adam Abram even if you never told any of us. I think if you believe you're mature enough to be a mother to a little girl, you can come to Thanksgiving with your family."

His words lanced through her heart so hard she winced, feeling physical pain.

For a moment the disapproving look left her brother's face, replaced by one of concern.

Every single day she battled against her fear at the thought of being a mom to Claire. She loved that little girl, loved the child's father too even if she'd never said the words out loud, but that didn't mean this was easy for her.

"Are you okay?" Jett asked.

Words were beyond her right now so she just nodded.

It wasn't true, of course, but maybe one day it could be.

The more time she spent with Adam, the more she believed in fairy-tales and the life he offered.

"If you're in trouble you can tell me, you know that don't you?" Jett asked his voice softened now.

No.

She didn't know it.

If she told him that because of her youthful stupidity she was in danger for life, he'd only remind her just how very stupid she'd been. As if she didn't know that already.

When she said nothing, Jett sighed, the concern gone, back to being the judgmental older brother. "You're not coming, are you?"

Jasmine shook her head.

Even if she'd been having doubts this conversation had convinced her she was doing the right thing.

Jett turned and walked toward his car.

The distance between her and her family hurt. She didn't like it, she just didn't believe knowing her story would change their opinion of her.

"It would help if you weren't all so judgmental," Jasmine blurted out.

Her big brother froze, turned slowly to face her, then looked over at the car where Savannah, his pregnant wife, and two-year-old son were sitting. She knew her brother had made mistakes that had almost cost him the woman he loved. "We all make mistakes, Jassy. The important thing is we learn from them."

"I learned," she murmured. Boy, had she learned.

"Then why don't you ever spend time with us?"

"Because I'm afraid that if you know what happened you won't just not like me, you all won't love me anymore." The admission hurt, and it was the first time she'd said it out loud, but it brought with it a sense of freedom.

Jett closed the distance between them, picked her up, and hugged her hard. "Nothing in the world could make us not love you, Jassy. Thanks for telling me what you need from us. I'll make sure we give it to you so you're sitting around the table next Thanksgiving."

With that, he set her on her feet and walked back to his car, driving off, leaving her staring open-mouthed after him.

Did that really just happen?

Had her admission led to her brother offering an olive branch?

A smile filled her face as she turned to head back inside, but it slid away when goosebumps broke out across her skin.

It felt like someone was watching her.

Quickly, she turned back around, expecting to find that Jett had come back for something.

But no one was there.

Carefully, she scanned the woods surrounding her cottage, but she couldn't see anyone, and nothing moved indicating a presence.

Nerves.

It was probably just leftover anxiety from Jett's visit.

Her cell phone rang, and she turned, forgetting the odd sensation as she closed and locked her door and hurried to get the phone. In the kitchen, Fauna looked up from where she was busy playing with a squeaky beaver toy as though she, too, knew who would be on the other end of the phone.

"Happy Thanksgiving," Adam said as soon as she answered.

"Happy Thanksgiving to you, too. Are you guys having fun?"

"We are, but it would be better if you were here."

Adam had invited her to spend Thanksgiving with him, Claire, and their family, but she wasn't ready for that yet. Maybe if it was just the three of them but not with all of his family. She'd met them all, and they were very nice, but a child's birthday party where everyone was running about, busy keeping the kids happy and entertained, was different. Thanksgiving dinner would involve talking, and she couldn't do that yet, nor could she ask him to not see his family and spend the day with her.

"Next year you will be though," Adam continued, the utter confidence in his tone making her mouth drop open for the second time in almost as many minutes.

For years she had spent the holiday—every holiday—alone, and now she'd had two people insist she would celebrate with them next year. It was surreal but also scary.

Because if they knew the truth, those offers would be rescinded and she'd be alone, not just for the holidays but forever.

CHAPTER
Ten

December 4th
4:47 P.M.

"Why are we so sure she's *not* a runaway?" Jessica asked.

Adam couldn't give a great answer to that question. It was more of a gut feeling than specifically based on fact.

More often than not his gut proved to be correct. Besides, this wasn't something worth risking.

"You want to do nothing when we know that she might not have left home by choice?" he asked his partner.

Jessica immediately shook her head. "Nope. I'd rather know we did everything we could, and if she did just run away then at least she knows someone cared enough to look for her."

"Exactly. Besides, it's what I'd want someone to do if it was Claire." Not that he could ever imagine his sweet little daughter running away, but who knows what teenage Claire would be like. Just because his life was pretty perfect at the moment, didn't mean that something awful couldn't happen.

"Ditto. If Freddie ever ran away, I'd want to know the cops took it seriously. And you're right, Karen Hopman doesn't have a history of running, nor does it look like she has a bad homelife or problems at school. If she did run of her own accord, there has to be a reason and that bears looking into anyway."

"Agreed." Adam glanced at his watch and winced. "I'm going to have to organize someone to watch Claire. The sitter has to leave at five thirty sharp, and my parents left on their cruise last night." It was one of the hardest things about working a job like his with unpredictable hours and being a single father. A late night wasn't as easy as just calling or texting to let his wife know he'd be late and to give their kids extra good-night kisses if he wasn't home by bedtime.

"My parents took Freddie on an overnight impromptu camping trip or they'd watch her," Jessica said. "Who are you going to call?"

"I was thinking Jasmine." While she hadn't babysat before, she'd spent lots of time with Claire over the last several months, and if he thought she'd say yes he'd ask her to move in with them permanently. Baby steps. As hard as that was to abide by sometimes, he knew that the only way to continue gaining Jasmine's trust was by taking things slow. He was pretty sure he already had her love or was at least close, but he wanted that elusive trust as well.

"You guys are a really cute couple," Jessica teased. His partner had been supportive of his growing relationship with Jasmine from the beginning, babysitting Claire a few times so he could take Jasmine out on dates.

"I know it's her busy time of year, but hopefully she can take a few hours off." It was a lot to ask, he got that, but he wanted someone he trusted to look after his daughter, and Jasmine was right up there on that list.

"Why don't you call, and I'll let the Hopman family know we're on our way."

While his partner did that, Adam snatched up his cell phone from his desk and walked over to an empty interview room. Bringing up his contacts, he found Jasmine's name and paused for a moment to stare at the photo he used for her. It was one he'd snapped over the summer where Jasmine had her arm around Claire as she pointed out a fox they'd spotted while on a hike. Behind them the sky was that deep, vivid blue of summer, and the sun was streaming down on them both. Their expressions were filled with wonder and delight, and the angle of the picture made it look like they were both looking off into the future.

Every time he looked at this picture he liked it more, and he'd actually had it printed onto a canvas to give to Jasmine as a Christmas gift. He'd had a copy made for him, too, and he couldn't wait to put it up on his wall as soon as he'd given Jasmine hers.

"Adam, is everything okay?" Jasmine asked when he hit call and she answered on the second ring.

"Fine, I was just wondering if I could ask you a favor."

"A favor? Of course. What do you need?"

"Something came up at work, and my parents are out of town, and the sitter has to leave in a little over thirty minutes, so I was wondering if you could watch Claire until I get home."

"You want me to babysit?"

"I know it's a lot to ask. This is your busy time of year, so I understand if you can't leave the farm. Plus, it's a busy time of the evening with Claire. You'll need to do dinner, and maybe bath and tuck her in if I'm not there. You know her routine and what she likes to eat."

"Are you sure?"

"Of what?"

"Me babysitting. I've never done it before."

"Not on your own, but you've spent plenty of time with her, you know her, she knows you, and she'll be thrilled to see you."

"Umm, well, yes, I guess I can. I mean, I can leave here. Everything runs like clockwork, and I'm mostly the behind-the-scenes person anyway. I was only catching up on correspondence which I can do later when I get home."

"Thank you so much. I owe you, big time."

"I guess I better get thinking of how you can repay me then," she teased.

Even though he knew she didn't mean it that way because they hadn't done more than some kissing and a little touching through clothing, Adam's mind immediately took the dirty route. While she was absolutely worth the wait, it didn't mean he wasn't looking forward to getting his gorgeous girl into bed and showing her how much he loved her and her delectable body.

"You do that, green eyes," he said.

From the way she sucked in a breath of air, Adam knew that her mind had taken the same train of thought his had.

Maybe his beautiful woman was a little closer to being ready to take that next step than he'd thought she was.

Now he couldn't wait to get home, tuck Claire in if he made it in time, and then spend some time showing Jasmine just how grateful he was not just because she babysat for him but just to have her in his life.

CHAPTER
Eleven

December 4th
5:29 P.M.

One minute to spare.

Jasmine quickly locked her car and hurried up the path to Adam's front door, giving a sharp knock.

A moment later, it was opened by the sitter, bouncing at her feet was a very excited Claire.

"You're here," Claire squealed, zooming in for a hug.

"Just in time, sorry about that, traffic," she said to the sitter as she returned Claire's hug.

"No problem," the woman assured her. "Normally I could stay later, but my granddaughter's recital is tonight."

"That sounds like fun. Do I need to pay you or has Adam already done that?" she asked. She hadn't thought to check and make sure the woman had been paid for her hours and had no idea of the arrangement Adam had with her for that.

"All good. He transfers the money into my account on the weeks I work looking after this cutie." The sitter tweaked one of Claire's pigtails, making the girl giggle.

"Enjoy the recital," Jasmine told the woman as she picked up her purse and headed out to her car.

"I want smashed potatoes and your chicken for dinner," Claire announced, grabbing her hand and dragging her inside.

"I think we can manage that."

"Can I help?" Claire bounced up and down with all the enthusiasm of a five-year-old.

"Course you can. I always like having my best helper around."

"I wish you could have dinner with me every day," Claire said, skipping on ahead to the kitchen.

The little girl didn't see it since Jasmine was behind her, but she froze at the child's casual statement.

Dinner with Claire and Adam every day?

In some ways it was a dream come true, in others it was her worst nightmare.

If there was one thing she knew for sure it was that she did not deserve to be a mother. She'd been there once before and had failed her baby in the worst possible way.

If she had failed her own tiny baby girl, how could she not believe she would also fail Adam's sweet little girl?

"Jassy, come on," Claire said, snapping her out of her head.

"Sorry, sweetie," she said, pasting on a smile. So far she'd done okay with Claire, and she hadn't *wanted* to fail her daughter. It had been taken out of her hands. And while she would always lay part of the blame squarely on her own shoulders, logically, Jasmine knew it hadn't really been her fault.

As she collected potatoes from the pantry and checked to make sure there was chicken before she got started, Claire buzzed about getting in the way, how only a small child who wanted to help could. There was chicken in the fridge, so she didn't have to pop out to get some, and she already knew there would be breadcrumbs and spices because she'd made this meal for Adam and Claire before and it had become a favorite with the both of them.

"Jassy!" Claire suddenly said, her tone gone from excited to worried.

"What's wrong?"

"Iggle Wiggle."

"What about him?" She'd known the child long enough to know that Iggle Wiggle was a stuffed giraffe that Claire had been given at birth. It was her comfort item, and she rarely went anywhere without it.

"I don't know where he is." Claire looked stricken like not only did she not know where her beloved giraffe was, but it had just occurred to her that she hadn't even realized he wasn't with her.

"It's okay, sweetie. Come here." Lifting the little girl up, she set her on the counter and stood in front of her, the child's hands in hers. "When was the last time you saw him?"

"I can't 'member."

"Did you play with him when you got home from school?"

"No, I was too busy playin' puzzles with Mrs. Owens."

"Well, I bet you had him in bed last night, right?"

Claire's brown eyes lit up. "I sleeped in Daddy's bed last night 'cause the monster in my closet was being real loud."

"There's no such thing as monsters," Jasmine said automatically even as her brain refuted the statement. There *were* monsters, she knew, she'd spent two years trapped with one. They might not be big and hairy, but they existed.

"He's prolly in Daddy's room," Claire said, squiggling to get down.

Lifting the little girl down, together they ran up the stairs and down to the master bedroom. Jasmine hadn't been in it before. Usually, when she came over, they stayed downstairs or out in the backyard. She'd been in Claire's room plenty of times and used the upstairs bathroom, but she'd never seen Adam's room.

When she entered it, she couldn't help but smile. It was totally him. His style was minimalist, with only the furniture you absolutely needed, no knickknacks and pretty much nothing on the walls, which were all painted crisp white, setting off the dark wooden floorboards. His bedroom was no exception. There was the bed with a masculine wood frame and two nightstands, and that was it. She could see an open door led to a walk-in closet, and she knew there was a master bath so that must be through the closet.

The only exception to the bare walls were two framed photos on the wall opposite the bed. One was of a newborn Claire, the other was from Adam's wedding.

While Claire scrambled across the neatly made bed in search of her stuffed giraffe, Jasmine walked toward the picture in stunned silence.

Adam had talked a lot about his wife. He hadn't hidden that while he had loved Meredith with his whole heart and would have spent the rest of his life with her, she was gone and he was still alive. It had taken time, but she'd been gone for almost five years now and he was ready to find love again.

He'd talked about what she was like and Claire's personality quirks that reminded him of her mother, but he had never shown her a picture of Meredith.

Now she knew why.

Looking at the picture was like looking into a mirror.

She might as well have been Meredith's twin sister.

CHAPTER
Twelve

December 4th
8:17 P.M.

Home.

Was there a better word in the English language?

In any language?

Adam didn't think that there was.

It encompassed everything that made life worth living. Family, safety, peace, it was all wrapped up in that one little word.

As he climbed out of his car and saw Jasmine's sitting in his driveway, he couldn't not smile. He liked seeing her car here, liked knowing she was inside with his daughter. Hopefully, this is what their future was going to look like.

Maybe it was still too soon to be thinking that far ahead given Jasmine's assault last year, and whatever in her past had her hiding away, but he couldn't not think of it.

This was what he wanted, the three of them together.

That good mood evaporated as soon as he stepped through the

door. Jasmine was waiting for him, only it wasn't a kiss or even a hello that awaited him as a greeting. The first words out of her mouth about stopped his heart.

"We need to break up," Jasmine blurted out.

Shock rendered him speechless.

How had a simple couple of hours babysitting led to her wanting to end their relationship?

The fact that she was standing there, anxiously swaying from foot to foot, twisting her hands together tightly enough that her knuckles were white only added to his shock. What could have happened to put her on edge?

"Did Claire do something?" His daughter was a sweet and sassy little girl. She loved people, made friends easily, had the occasional tantrum, but mostly was good-natured and even-tempered. Still, it wasn't out of the realm of possibility that she had said or done something that had upset Jasmine.

Still wanting to break up seemed extreme.

Jasmine might have her issues, but she wasn't a drama queen. She was genuinely battling trauma yet still got up each day, ran her business, was always friendly and kind to Claire, and little by little let him in.

It was like he'd stepped into some sort of parallel universe.

"What? No! Of course not. Claire is just the sweetest little girl ever. I completely adore her."

"Then what happened?" Had he done something? What could he have done when he wasn't even here?

"N-nothing," she stammered, but she wouldn't meet his eye. "Claire wanted mashed potato and chicken for dinner. There's a plate for you in the fridge. I let her have some ice cream for dessert. I assume that was okay. She had a bath, we read some stories, and I tucked her in on time."

Frustration built inside him. "Don't act like you were here just as the babysitter and give me a rundown of the night."

"I *was* here as the babysitter."

"You were—are—here as my girlfriend."

"N-no. Not anymore. I ... I can't."

There was such misery in her voice, and her eyes brimmed with unshed tears, that his frustration fled. "Talk to me. What happened?"

Her gaze darted around the room, not settling on any one thing for more than about a second. "Claire couldn't find Iggle Wiggle. She said she had him in your room last night. I wasn't snooping, I swear, we only went up there so she could get her giraffe."

So she'd been in his bedroom, so what?

Why was she freaking out about that?

If she'd been more comfortable with intimacy that room would already be half hers.

"I don't mind you going into my room. I want you to feel comfortable here."

"I saw," Jasmine whispered.

He still wasn't following. "Saw what?"

"The picture."

"What picture."

"Of you and your wife."

"Okay," he said slowly. He had absolutely no idea what she was trying to tell him and why it had upset her so badly.

"Meredith, your wife, she looks just like me. You can't tell me you didn't know that. It's so obvious. Is that why you were so nice to me after I was assaulted because you saw your wife in me? Is that why you wanted to go out with me? Why you let me spend time with Claire? Do you want me to be a replacement for the wife that you lost?"

Her pained tirade didn't make him any less confused, but at least he knew what had her freaking out.

He guessed since she was already unsure about herself, it made sense she was upset, but honestly, she was upset about nothing.

Taking a tentative step toward her, he stopped when she darted sideways. "You and Meredith look a little alike sure. You're both blondes. I'm attracted to blondes. And sure, she had green eyes, too, but that's totally a coincidence. Other than that, you're just both beautiful young women. I promise you I'm not into you because I want you to try to be Meredith. You both have different personalities, you're different people. I like you both equally."

There was clear doubt on her face, and he had to assume it really had more to do with the secrets she continued to keep. Adam wasn't angry with her about it, she was entitled to her secrets, and they had only been together for a few months, friends for a year and a half. Whatever had happened to her, he didn't think she'd even told her family.

"I want to be with *you*, Jasmine. I want a future with you. I think I've been clear about that. If I didn't see a future with you, I wouldn't let you spend time with my daughter. Claire is my world, and I want to share her with you. I know you're going to be an amazing mom to her and an amazing partner to me."

Although he'd intended his words to be reassuring, Jasmine choked on a sob, then darted around him toward the door. "I'm sorry, I can't do this. I'm sorry, I'm so sorry."

Before he could stop her, she had bolted out the door and ran toward her car, leaving him staring after her wondering what had just happened.

Had they really just broken up?

Would Jasmine see sense when she calmed down?

And what had brought on this meltdown when he'd thought things between them were going so well?

CHAPTER
Thirteen

December 15th
9:32 A.M.

She was miserable.

Had she overreacted?

Jasmine knew that wasn't even really a question.

Of course, she had.

Panic.

She'd panicked.

It wasn't even really to do with the picture of Adam's wife. Sure, it had been a shock, and yeah, she'd had a moment where she had wondered if she was some sort of replacement, but in the end, it wasn't why she had bolted.

Nope.

The reason she had bolted was because she was a coward.

She ran when she should stand and fight.

This wasn't the first time she'd done that. Shame had kept her from properly reconnecting with her family after she'd managed to escape.

How could they love and forgive her, when she couldn't even love or forgive herself?

Then a few nights ago when she'd been babysitting Claire, she'd gotten a picture of what life could have been like if her daughter hadn't died. There wouldn't have been any picture-perfect life if she hadn't escaped. She knew what would have happened to her baby. It would either have been abandoned or sold, but knowing she was pregnant had tipped her hand, and she would have gotten out of the life she'd been trapped in.

Maybe if she had, she could have had the kind of life Adam was offering.

The kind of life she still struggled to believe that she deserved.

Jasmine felt like she was a basket case. Trapped. That's how she felt. Tied to the past because it wasn't completely in the past. There was still a threat hanging over her head. If he ever found her, he would kill her. It had always been a risk staying so close to home, but she'd thought he would be too scared to come back here and make a move on her if he even thought she would stay here. Likely he thought she had long since fled, and given it had been six years since she escaped and he hadn't come after her, he probably wouldn't ever find her.

But what if he did?

That thought hovered constantly at the back of her mind.

Could she stay with Adam knowing she might be putting him and his daughter at risk?

How would she survive knowing she was responsible for the death of a good man and his sweet little girl?

That wasn't the only thought hovering constantly in her mind. Should she tell Adam about her past? If she did, it would effectively end any chance they might get back together, but perhaps that wasn't the worst thing that could happen. Maybe she just wasn't cut out to be in a relationship. Or she could tell her brother. He was an FBI agent. He might be able to do something to end the threat to her once and for all.

It was probably the smart move, but that plan had a major roadblock.

It might mean losing everything.

Adam had fought for her so far, but would he continue to do so if he knew how stupid she'd been, the terrible things she'd done, and how she hadn't protected her unborn baby? Her big brother said her family would love her no matter what, that nothing could change that, but was it really true?

Sensing her emotions, Fauna nudged at her knee, licking her hand when she went to pet the dog. She was a big girl now, fully grown, mature, so very empathetic, and well trained. Jasmine had taken advantage of Adam's friend's offer to help her continue Fauna's training. While her girl might not have been a good police dog, she was an amazing guard dog. Young as she still was, she had taken to that training and was as protective as could be of Jasmine.

"It's okay, girl. I'll be okay," she assured the dog, determined to somehow make it true. "Ready to go back home?"

Finding a quiet place on her property at this time of year, a mere ten days away from Christmas was next to impossible, but this little spot where Adam had set up the campfire on their first date was her special spot. No one came here because it wasn't part of the public space, and her staff had no reason to be out there either. Coming out here wasn't a good idea, not if she wanted to get over Adam, but she couldn't seem to stay away these last few days since she'd made a clean break of things with Adam and Claire.

Now she stood, brushing a couple of leaves off her backside. She was chilled from sitting out on the cold ground, but she didn't care. It was kind of like her body just matched her heart.

With Fauna sticking close they made their way back to the house. As soon as she stepped inside Jasmine immediately felt like something was wrong.

Was someone here?

Quickly, she checked the door, but there was no sign that the lock had been picked or the door pried open. Not that that necessarily meant anything, someone could have broken in but not left any signs, or they could have come in the back door or any of the ground floor windows.

Panic flooded her system and short-circuited her brain.

Fight or flight, both seemed out of her reach right now, she was just frozen to the spot.

Had someone been in her home or was she imagining things? Was she letting her stressed-out mind get the best of her maybe?

"No one was in here," she said confidently as though she could manifest that into truth by speaking it aloud.

It had to be the truth. Already she was overloaded with thinking about the past and the future she'd given up when she walked away from Adam. She couldn't handle anything else.

Which was why she absolutely refused to acknowledge the possibility that her past might have finally caught up to her and she might be about to pay for the sins she had committed with her very life.

CHAPTER
Fourteen

December 15th
10:03 A.M.

"Daddy!"

"Hey, pumpkin, watch your attitude," Adam rebuked his daughter. Ever since Jasmine had walked away ten days ago Claire had been struggling.

Actually, he had been too.

He'd tried reaching out to her to get her to talk to him, but she wouldn't answer his calls or respond to his texts, and he was starting to get desperate.

Even though he'd fight for her—had been fighting for her—he had to accept that it might not work out the way he wanted it to. It wouldn't be anyone's fault. Jasmine couldn't help that she had issues and traumas to deal with, but he also couldn't make her ready to confront them.

She had to want to do it.

Not for him, not for Claire, not for anyone but herself.

It was the only way to truly heal.

That was what he wanted for her.

As much as he understood that Claire was hurting and confused, same as him, he couldn't allow her to act out because of it. Talking through her feelings was fine, but being disrespectful absolutely was not.

"Sorry, Daddy," Claire said contritely.

"That's okay. What's up?"

"I drew a picture for Jassy. I want to take it to her," Claire said firmly. They'd already had a talk about Jasmine not coming around as much. Since he wasn't ready to put a full stop to their story, he'd phrased it more as a comma. Adam had told his daughter that Jasmine was upset and needed a little space, kind of like a grown-up time-out. That explanation seemed to have worked for the last couple of days, but now she was getting antsy.

"We can't right now."

Claire stomped her foot. "But I want to. And I want Jassy's chicken for dinner."

"I can make you that."

"You don't make it as good as Jassy does. I want *her* to make it."

"I'd love for her to make you chicken and have dinner with us, but she can't. Not tonight." Maybe not any night but he wasn't going to say that to his daughter.

"Please."

Adam smiled ruefully. "Please doesn't work all the time, pumpkin."

"Can it work this time?"

"Come here, baby." Pushing away from the kitchen table where he'd been working while Claire drew, he reached over and picked up his little girl, setting her on his lap. "It's not that Jasmine doesn't like you anymore or wants to make you sad or even angry. Jasmine had something bad happen to her, and she just needs some time to think about it."

"Something bad?" Claire asked.

"Someone hurt her, and sometimes after we get hurt, we get scared of being hurt again. Like, remember when you were on the swing and you forgot to hold on and fell off? After that, you were scared to go on the swing again for a long time."

"But, Daddy, you made me go back on the swing. You said if you fall off the giraffe, you got to get right back on," Claire told him, giving him a smug look like she was pleased with herself.

"Horse, pumpkin," he said, chuckling at her substituting her favorite animal.

"I like giraffes better. They have long necks so theys can see *everywhere*."

"I didn't make you get back on right away though," he reminded her.

"But you did make me. You said you'd given me nuff time and I had to face my scareds."

"I said that, huh?" he asked thoughtfully.

"Uh-huh, that's what you said, and you're a daddy so you knows everything."

"Hmm," he said as his mind spun with ideas. He had given Jasmine time to figure things out on her own, maybe she needed a little push. She'd opened up a bit with him about her relationship with her family, and he knew she kept her distance because she thought they wouldn't love her if they knew the truth about her.

That they also kept their distance reinforced her ideas.

Convinced her that she wasn't worth their effort.

Was him giving her too much space showing her the same thing?

"I guess we could call Jasmine, just say hi, tell her you drew her this beautiful picture."

"We's playing the piano," Claire informed him. "Jassy still has to teached me to play songs."

"Let's call her and tell her." Grabbing his cell phone from the counter, he lifted Claire up and set her down then put the phone on speaker. Jasmine likely wouldn't answer, but at least she'd get the message.

"Jassy!" Claire said excitedly when her voicemail picked up. "I drew you a picture. It's you and me, and we're playing piano. You still got to give me lessons." There was a reprimand to Claire's tone that made him smile.

"We miss you, green eyes. Both of us. We hope you're okay, and we hope you know how much we care about you."

"And we loves you," Claire added.

"And we love you," he echoed, hoping Jasmine knew that even though this was the first time he'd said it out loud he'd felt this way for a long time now. "We're not letting you get away, are we, pumpkin?"

"Nope. Because Jassy is ours and we're hers."

"Couldn't have said it better myself. We'll talk soon, green eyes. Love you. Bye."

"Bye, I love you!" Claire chimed in before he ended the call. "I was a good match girl," she said proudly.

"A match girl?"

"You said match girls help people fall in love," Claire explained.

"Matchmaker, and right. That's exactly what they do, and you're very good at it."

"Can we post my picture to Jassy if we can't go see her?"

"Sure. I'm sure I have an envelope around here somewhere."

"Can you show me some words to write on there?"

"Absolutely. What do you want to write?"

"I want to write Jassy's name, and I want to say I love you, and that I want her to be my new mommy. That's what I askeded Santa for."

His heart melted right then and there.

When he lost Meredith, he hadn't been ready to think of moving on one day, but over time as the pain dulled and he started to think he might want to meet someone, fall in love and get married again, he could only hope his daughter would love that person, and that they'd love Claire in return.

He'd lucked out with Jasmine.

If she could find the courage to face down her demons, then all three of them could be happy together. She had him and his little match girl at her back, all she needed to do was reach out to them and they'd be there.

CHAPTER
Fifteen

December 15th
6:55 P.M.

Physical exhaustion was the only thing getting her by right now.

Jasmine had thrown herself into her work, not a hard thing to do ten days before Christmas. Other than a couple of times a day when she'd sneak away to go to what she now thought of as her and Adam's spot, she worked.

And worked.

And worked.

Worked until her body and mind were so worn out that she was able to collapse and go to sleep.

The farm wouldn't close until ten tonight, but she had to pop back to her place to check on Fauna. Since her dog didn't like being in crowds, Jasmine usually left her at home. She had a small fenced-in yard and a doggie door so Fauna could go inside or outside, whatever she chose. Usually, she hung out inside. The kitchen was free range for her if Jasmine wasn't home, and when she was there her dog was allowed to wander throughout the house with her. More often than not, Fauna was by her side.

A true companion.

Honestly, she didn't know how she would have gotten through this last year and a half without the dog.

That Adam had known what she needed when even she didn't know and gone out and done something about it was just another tick in the pro column when it came to her internal debate on whether or not she should ask him for another chance.

Trying to figure it out was exhausting in and of itself, and it felt like running in a circle, like Fauna when she was a puppy trying to chase her own tail.

What she needed was help.

Real help.

It might be the only shot she ever had at having a future.

What she was doing now clearly wasn't working and continuing to do it when she knew that and expecting things to change would be insanity.

Doing the same thing over and over and expecting a different result.

That was the definition of insanity, and she wanted so badly to break out of that cycle.

As she pulled up outside her place, leaving her car out front rather than putting it in the garage since she'd be going back out after a check-in with Fauna, Jasmine pulled out her phone.

For someone who never used to get any calls or texts from anyone who wasn't associated with her business, her phone had been blowing up these last few weeks. Every single person in her family, her mom and all six of her brothers and sisters, had been reaching out to her constantly. Nothing major just saying hi, telling some funny anecdote of something that had happened to them, or sending a joke. Her mom had been sending some inspirational messages people always shared on social media.

Whatever Jett had said to them on Thanksgiving had made a difference. It was like they were trying to show her that she was still part of them.

She *didn't* feel part of them anymore, it had been so long since she had left. Back then she'd been a sixteen-year-old kid, naïve, with no idea how the world worked, and no idea what lay beyond the relative safety of her home.

Now she knew.

Been irrevocably changed by that evil.

Which brought her to Adam and Claire. They kept reaching out to her, too. They'd left her a message earlier telling her that they loved her.

Loved her.

It was so shocking to her, but it also made her think.

She had to get help.

Without it, she was leaving herself willingly floundering lost in the middle of the ocean. That wasn't where she wanted to spend the rest of her life. She wanted to feel safe again, get her feet back on solid ground, and wanted to belong. She was so tired of being alone.

Holding her phone tightly in her hand as though it possessed the power to save her, Jasmine climbed out of her SUV and headed for her front door. Kisses and cuddles with her girl were what she needed right now, then she'd finish out her work for the day and tomorrow ... tomorrow maybe she'd look up some local counselors and get herself the help she needed.

Jasmine knew as soon as she opened the front door that something was wrong.

It was too quiet.

Odd because her dog wasn't a barker so it was always quiet when she got home, but this quiet felt different.

It felt empty.

Her house was never empty when she got home because Fauna was always there. Sometimes she gave a little whimper for a welcome, but her presence was always there.

Today it wasn't.

The lights were on because they were always on. She had them set to a timer so they came on as soon as it got dark, and she saw something lying on the floor in the middle of the hall.

Don't go to it.

Leave.

Something's wrong.

Her internal voice gave her sensible instructions, and yet she walked toward what looked like a picture anyway. Maybe it was the drawing Claire had been talking about in the voicemail.

When she reached it, she stooped down and picked it up.

Immediately, she realized her mistake in not running as soon as she grasped something was wrong.

The picture was hers. It was a sonogram of her baby from the day she found out she was pregnant. It was all she had left of her daughter. She kept it tucked away in a small box in the nightstand beside her bed.

Someone had been in her home.

Gone through her things.

Left it here for her to find.

There was only one person who it could be.

Bobby Johnson.

Her personal bogeyman.

The man she once believed she was in love with.

Back when she was young and stupid. But he stole her youth, her innocence, her family, her daughter, and maybe even her future.

"I've been waiting for this."

At the sound of the voice, Jasmine jolted to her feet, spinning around to find him standing by her front door, closing it, and locking it behind him.

Locking her in here with him.

Even if she'd left as soon as she realized something was wrong, he would have gotten her. He'd come for her, there was no way he was leaving without getting what he wanted.

"It's been a long time, Jasmine. Too long. You thought you got away from me. Almost did, too. I didn't think you'd be stupid enough to stay here. I've been looking for you in the wrong place. Until you killed a man. Lucky for me I have someone in the department who alerted me to your presence here. Thought you were smart, didn't you? Using a different name for the farm, hiding out here, but I have you now, and this time, I'm never letting you go."

When he took a step toward her, she ran.

But just like when she'd been a kid, he was bigger, stronger, and on her in seconds.

Spinning her around, he slammed her back up against the nearest wall, his large hands clamped around her throat.

How many times had he had her in this same position?

Too many to recall.

Bobby wasn't leaving here without her. She couldn't fight him off, her only hope was to leave behind something for someone to find and pray that they figured out who had taken her.

Lifting her hands, she clawed at his arms. It was part instinctual since those arms were attached to his hands which were squeezing the life out of her, and part the only hope she had to leave a clue behind. Scraping her fingernails down his arms hard enough to draw blood, she used that blood to write his initials on the sonogram she still held.

His hands were squeezing.

Her vision began to fade.

A rushing sound like waves filled her ears.

The sonogram picture fluttered to the floor.

The world around her turned black.

CHAPTER
Sixteen

December 16th
8:12 A.M.

Adam hoped coming here wasn't a mistake.

There had been no reply to the message he and Claire had left yesterday or to the one he'd left her late last night, but something was urging him to come here.

Not one to argue with the universe, after dropping Claire off at her school he'd driven straight over to the farm. As he approached Jasmine's house it looked quiet, peaceful, and yet he got an edgy feeling.

Something felt wrong, but nothing looked wrong.

Still, his gut told him things for a reason, and as he parked his vehicle and got out, he let his hand hover over his weapon. If nothing was going on he didn't want to scare or upset Jasmine, but if there was something untoward happening, he wanted to be prepared.

Even before he climbed the porch steps, he knew he was right.

The sound of Fauna whimpering and crying in the backyard told him something was wrong.

That dog was practically glued to Jasmine's side. When she was out, she let the dog have the use of the fenced yard and the kitchen by use of a doggie door. At this time in the morning, Jasmine should still be at home, and even if she'd left to take care of something for her farm the dog wouldn't be crying in the yard, she'd either be out enjoying the fresh air or hanging inside. Knowing Fauna, likely inside playing with one of her toys.

Pulling his gun free, Adam climbed the porch steps and found the front door open.

Weapon in hand, he entered Jasmine's home, still desperately hoping that whatever was wrong was minor. Maybe she'd just had a fall and was unable to get to her phone to call for help. Wasn't like that would be a good thing but certainly better than the alternative.

Because the alternative was that she had been taken from her home by force, or she'd been hurt—or killed—by whoever had broken in.

But her home was empty.

He cleared it room by room and found nothing.

No signs of Jasmine.

In the kitchen, he did find something disturbing. On the floor of her pantry, there was a blanket and a pillow. Had Jasmine been sleeping down here? For how long? Was this a result of her assault or to do with her past?

It broke his heart to know she closed herself in the pantry at night in an attempt to feel safe.

But as upsetting as it was, he had bigger issues to deal with now.

Grabbing his phone, Adam called Jessica. "I need a team at Jasmine Crane's house now," he said without preamble.

"What's wrong?"

"I got here and the front door was open, dog was locked out the back, and no signs of Jasmine."

"I'll be right there and make sure a CSU team is sent right out. Any idea who took her or why?"

"No. But she's keeping some sort of secret about her past. I'll call her brother and see if he knows what it might be." As he talked to his partner, he went to the back door and opened it, letting Fauna in.

Maybe the dog could point him in a direction, any direction, so long as he had something to work with.

No way was he losing Jasmine like this.

As soon as she was inside, Fauna darted around him and ran into the hall. She walked right down to a spot and stopped, looking straight at him and whining.

"Hold on, the dog might have something." Because animals were intuitive and Fauna was the closest thing he had to a witness, he went to see what the dog was trying to tell him and found something half hidden under a chair, like it had been dropped and fluttered down to rest there. When he picked it up he saw it was a sonogram picture.

Even before he looked at it, he knew this was the reason Jasmine was so hesitant to let anyone in. They hadn't had sex so he knew the baby wasn't his, and her rape was well over a year ago. This pregnancy was part of her past.

"Find anything?" Jessica asked.

"A picture of a sonogram. Date on it says it's six years old." Which meant Jasmine's baby would be close in age to Claire. How hard must it have been for her to be around his daughter when her heart must have been aching for her own child. He had no idea if she'd lost the baby or given it up for adoption, but either way, she was a mother without her baby.

"I'll look into Jasmine's life at that time, try to identify a possible father."

"Wait. There's something else." On the back of the picture were two letters which looked to be written in blood.

A clue.

While his girl had been fighting for her life—because he knew Jasmine was at heart a fighter—she had also been thinking ahead. Trying to leave something behind so he'd have a way to find her.

Hold on, green eyes. I'm coming.

"It's letters on the back of the picture. B J."

"I'll start running the initials and see if they pop anything."

"I'm going to call Jett, see if we can access some of the FBI's resources, and see what he knows about his sister's life six years ago and who she knew with the initials B J."

"Good luck."

After he hung up he gave Fauna a pat. If the dog hadn't drawn his attention to the picture it might not have been discovered until CSU went through the place. Hours. They might have wasted hours.

Finding Jett Crane's number, Adam called it.

"Hello?" Jett said.

"This is Adam Abram. I'm standing in your sister's house," he said.

"What's wrong?" the other man asked immediately.

"I don't know. I got here and the place was empty, front door open, dog locked out."

"I'm on my way," Jett said immediately.

"She left behind a clue for us," Adam told Jasmine's brother as he could hear the man moving about. "It's a sonogram picture."

"Jasmine doesn't have a kid."

"Well, she has a sonogram picture dated six years ago."

Jett sucked in a breath. "Eight years ago Jasmine disappeared. Completely. No signs of her, no contact, nothing. She was gone for two years. When she was eighteen she made contact, told us she was okay, but wouldn't talk about those two years, and kept her distance."

"Do the initials B J mean anything to you?"

"B J? There was a man when Jassy was sixteen. I had already moved out long before then, but I remember Mom was upset about this man Jas wanted to date. She thought he was too old for her. She was sixteen, he was twenty-seven. Jas claimed she was in love with him, when she ran we all thought it was to be with him. Bobby Johnson. B J."

Now it was Adam's turn to suck in a breath. He knew that name. It had come up in a recent investigation into a missing teenager.

The man was rumored to be a pimp who took teenage girls by force and coerced them into working for him.

CHAPTER
Seventeen

December 16th
11:04 A.M.

Pain drummed through her body, thrumming a steady beat.

It weighed heavily upon her, making it hard to think of anything else.

Jasmine knew she shouldn't be surprised that Bobby was taking such pleasure in beating her, but for some reason she was.

Too much time had passed and the events, while still in her mind, were less vivid than they'd been when she first escaped. Time had dulled the terror and allowed her to become complacent. It had turned Bobby Johnson from a very real monster who had ruined her life, to a distant kind of bogeyman, still real, still dangerous, but she had been distracted by other things.

Things she'd never get a chance to fix.

There might not—likely wouldn't be—an opportunity to tell Adam that she had been planning on getting professional help so she could be who he and Claire needed her to be. Or tell her family she was sorry for being stupid and selfish, and that she hadn't stayed away for two years because she wanted to, but because she was unable to go home.

Her life would very likely end in this room.

She had no idea where she was or how far away from home she'd been taken because Bobby had moved her while she was unconscious. When she woke, she'd been in this room, chained to the wall. Her throat ached, and she was sure if she looked in a mirror it would be marred with black fingerprint-sized bruises.

Not the first time it had been.

Not the first time her entire body had been covered in bruises.

Jasmine looked down her body, he'd stripped her naked while she'd been unconscious, and now her skin was littered with black and blue marks.

Beating her into submission was just one way he had ensured she complied with his orders, the other was threats. Not just to herself and what would happen to her if she tried to leave, but threats to her family as well.

If it were just her life on the line, she would have risked it, but risking the lives of her two younger sisters? That she couldn't do.

So, she'd stayed in hell.

Endured life as a prostitute as penance for her stupidity, and the only way she knew how to keep her baby sisters from being subjected to the horrors her life had become. Daily beatings, starved, kept locked in a tiny bedroom with nothing but a mattress on the floor, a crude toilet, and a showerhead embedded in the wall that had only cold water. Raped more days than not by men who paid her pimp money, money which never came to her.

It was all for Bobby.

She was nothing but a prop to make him rich while she lived in worse conditions than most animals.

One chance.

That was all she'd had to escape him, and she'd taken it.

There wouldn't be another.

This was it.

Even if someone was able to decipher the meager clue she'd been able to leave behind, that didn't mean they would find her. She could be anywhere, and she didn't even know when someone would discover she'd been abducted.

Would they even think that she'd been taken against her will?

Her family already believed she was immature and selfish, they might just think she'd bailed. And she'd broken Adam's heart—Claire's too—when she left. He'd been nothing but patient with her, working to earn her trust, fighting for her, for them, and she'd repaid him by bailing because she'd let her insecurities get the best of her.

Maybe he'd think she just left too.

Irresponsible Jasmine.

Selfish Jasmine.

Doesn't love and care about anyone but herself Jasmine.

That's what everyone thought of her. Maybe no one would even care that she was gone.

No one but Fauna.

Was her sweet doggie okay?

Had Bobby hurt her?

She would ask when he came back, but she was terrified if he knew just how much she loved that dog he'd go back and get it out of spite so he could use it against her, threaten to hurt it as a way to manipulate her.

The door to the basement where she was chained to the wall was opened, and Bobby slowly descended the stairs. He looked the same as he had the last time she'd seen him six years ago. His dark hair was still free of gray, there were no wrinkles on his face, and his bright blue eyes —eyes that had once captivated her and made her believe she'd fallen in love—were just as bright, only now she saw the darkness they held.

Dressed as he usually was, he wore a pair of black jeans and a crisp white shirt with the sleeves rolled up to the elbows. His arms were muscled and strong, and she knew he spent hours a day working out. At one time she'd liked that he was so big and strong, it had made her feel safe and protected. Little did she know how easily he could use that size and strength against her.

Now she knew though.

Knew as he gave her that one-sided smirk she'd once found sexy that he was about to deliver another beating.

As much as she wanted to beg for mercy, she knew it was pointless. He liked that, he liked knowing that you were terrified of him. It made him feel like some sort of god.

"Are you ready?" he asked as he stood before her.

Even knowing what was coming, Jasmine couldn't make herself say the words he wanted to hear.

"Still being defiant? You were the one who ran, even knowing what would happen if you did. You were the one who was selfish, and yet I never went after your sisters, did I?"

Bobby said it as though he'd done her a favor by not abducting her little sisters like he'd told her he would if she ever disobeyed him.

He'd done it for himself not for her.

For her to go missing and then her sisters, it would bring too much attention to her family, attention that could easily turn to him. She'd gone into hiding, not seen anyone those first few months as she slowly healed from the injuries that had almost stolen her life along with her unborn baby's. Bobby likely knew if he went after her sisters she would go to the cops and tell them everything.

Selfish.

He was always selfish.

She would never thank him for anything, he'd destroyed her life, her sense of self, her entire identity.

"You think you can hold out now but how long can you really last? Sooner or later, you'll be on your knees before me performing the job I taught you to do and thanking me for my generosity."

As the first blow landed directly in her stomach, shoving the air from her lungs, Jasmine knew she would never give Bobby what he wanted.

It was either be rescued or die here in this room.

Those were her only options.

CHAPTER
Eighteen

December 16th
4:27 P.M.

"Are we sure this is it?" Adam asked as they pulled up outside what looked like a completely normal and nondescript family home in a decent suburb. The area wasn't a wealthy one, there were no mansions and fancy cars parked in driveways, but neither was it impoverished. Just your average, middle-class neighborhood.

It certainly didn't look like a house where a pimp held teenage girls prisoner and forced them to prostitute themselves.

According to Karen Hopman, a teenager who had been initially reported as a runaway, but had been proven to have been abducted, this was where she had been brought by the older man she thought was her boyfriend. The teen had told them she hadn't run away, she'd just gone to spend the day with Bobby Johnson, her thirty-five-year-old boyfriend. Only when she got there he had informed her that she was not permitted to leave and that he owned her now.

The girl hadn't understood what he meant or what was going on, and when she'd told him she wasn't going to prostitute herself and was going home he'd viciously beaten her.

That beating had saved her life.

Even though Bobby had threatened to go after Karen's little sister and force her into prostitution if she refused, the teenager had reached out for help at the hospital.

If it hadn't been for Karen, he wouldn't have known who Bobby was or been able to track down the house where the teenager had been taken.

He also wouldn't have known what Jasmine had been too ashamed to tell him.

That she had also fallen for Bobby's ruse, only she had heeded the threats to her younger sisters and stayed with the violent pimp for two years. Likely the only thing that eventually allowed her to break free was the fact that she'd wound up pregnant.

Jasmine would have to tell him the specifics, but he could make a guess on how it happened.

"According to what Karen told us this has to be it," Jessica replied.

"I hope she's in there," he said as they both got out of their vehicle. If Bobby hadn't brought her here, he had no idea where to look next. Every second Jasmine was with this violent psychopath was another moment she was being hurt.

Because there was no way this man had waited six years to get his hands on her and hadn't hurt her.

Sending up a quick prayer, Adam and Jessica made their way to the front door. They had no idea if this was where Bobby based his prostitution business or if this was a private home. Karen had only been in the living room and kitchen when she was here, so she wasn't aware if other girls were also being held prisoner on the premises.

The house was quiet as they entered. According to Karen, there had been no other men here, nor had she seen any others hanging around when she met up with Bobby. They assumed that he ran the show himself, less people to split the money with, but they still carefully cleared each room on the ground floor.

Finding no one, they headed up the stairs.

As soon as they reached the second floor, Adam knew the house wasn't empty.

Each of the doors up here had a padlock on the outside, and all four of those padlocks were currently locked.

There was also a bedroom being used by a male, and a bathroom that looked like it hadn't been used in a while, both of which were empty.

They had to be here.

Adam couldn't accept another option.

"I'm calling backup before we let them out. If Bobby is here, they're safer in their rooms," Jessica said although he could tell it pained her to leave what were likely teenage girls locked in rooms unaware they were safe now and minutes away from being rescued.

"There was a door in the kitchen. It could lead to a basement," he said, unwilling to accept that Jasmine wasn't here somewhere counting on him to find her.

Jessica nodded, and while she put in a quick call to get more cops on the scene, they headed back downstairs. As soon as they opened the door in the corner of the kitchen, Adam knew he was right.

Jasmine and Bobby were down there.

The unmistakable sound of flesh hitting flesh had him seeing red.

Knowing it was his girl being hit had his blood boiling.

However much time she needed he'd give her, but he and Jasmine were going to get their happy ever after.

With his partner on his heels, he took the stairs two at a time.

When they reached the bottom, Bobby Johnson turned to stare at them. His knuckles were bloodied as was the front of his white shirt. There was shock on his face that quickly morphed into fury.

Chained to the wall was a naked Jasmine.

Bruises littered her body along with splatters of blood.

Bobby gave them a wicked smile and reached into his pocket.

There was no way he was hesitating when he had no idea whether or not Bobby was armed, and Jasmine's life was on the line.

Adam fired.

Hit his target a split second after Bobby pulled out a weapon.

Leaving Jessica to check that the man was dead, Adam focused solely on the woman he loved.

Snatching up a key that hung nearby, he unlocked both of Jasmine's ankles and then one of her wrists and draped her arm over his shoulder.

"I got you, baby," he murmured. Balancing her with an arm around her waist, he unlocked her other wrist and gathered her up against his chest.

"Adam," she whispered, her voice laden with pain. "You came."

"Nowhere in the world I wouldn't go for you, green eyes. I'll fight for you forever if I have to. Anything to make you mine."

Although both her eyes were swollen half shut, and one of her lips was split, a small smile lit her face. "You're not fighting alone. I promise not to give up again. I'll fight for us, too."

Nothing she could have said would have made him happier than those words.

CHAPTER
Nineteen

December 17th
5:35 P.M.

"I think your brother wanted to beat me up when you said you were coming home with me," Adam teased as he helped her out of the wheelchair and over to his truck.

Jasmine had wanted to argue against the wheelchair. Hospital policy or not, it kind of felt like a weakling move to use it, but even though she'd wanted to rebel against the notion that she needed it, needed anything, the reality was she felt awful. Her entire body was a mass of black and blue. She had a couple of cracked ribs, a hairline fracture in her left forearm, and some bruising to her internal organs in her abdomen.

It was going to be a long and painful recovery, but things could have been so much worse.

"Jett wouldn't have. He knew I was where I wanted to be. He can just be a bit of a control freak." She arched a brow at him.

"Hey, are you implying I am also a control freak?" Adam mock pouted, and she giggled then immediately sucked in a pained breath.

"Note to self: no laughing for a while," she said, bracing her good arm around her ribs.

"Sorry, sweetheart," Adam said as he carefully scooped her up and set her in the passenger seat. He buckled her in as though she were a child, then rounded the car and got in the driver's seat.

The drive to his house was quiet, but the kind of content and companionable silence, and Jasmine knew she'd made the right choice. Going home alone would have been silly and given that she'd been attacked and abducted there she wasn't sure she ever wanted to go back and live there. Already she'd been sleeping in the pantry because it was small. She could lock herself in, and no intruder would look for her there. What more could she do to feel safe?

Nothing.

This was where she felt safe.

"We're home, honey," Adam announced, and she glanced out the window to see his house.

"Home," she echoed.

"Sorry, I know this isn't your ..."

"No, what you said is perfect. It hasn't been my home, but maybe one day it could be." It was what she wanted. Jasmine was done hiding from her past and the mistakes that she'd made. They were done, she'd made them, there was no taking them back, and the consequences were still ones she lived with on a daily basis, but maybe there was a way to move forward, to have a future.

She wanted that future so badly.

It was scary and wouldn't be easy, but she'd survived a lot, and she could do whatever it took to make peace with the past. Jasmine had the best motivation in the world to do just that and one half of it was sitting beside her right now.

Adam and Claire were worth the hard work it would take to be who they needed.

Reaching out, his large hands closed gently around her good one. "I want this to be your home as soon as you're ready. Once you're healed if you need space, you take it."

"I tried space, I tried cutting everyone out, it didn't work." Admitting your failures wasn't always easy, but she owed this man who had proven over and over again that he was trustworthy, that she could depend on him, nothing but the truth.

"I'm here for you."

"I know."

"Claire too."

Tears blurred her vision. That little girl was both a blessing and a curse. She was a reminder of what Jasmine had lost when she lost her baby, but also a reminder of what could still be.

"I'm so sorry, green eyes. I know about your loss. I hate that you had to go through that." The hand that held hers squeezed tightly, and she felt everything he was trying to convey.

"Bobby said he was giving us birth control. I didn't even know I was pregnant until that day." This wasn't a story she had shared before, but it was time. Time to honor her daughter who never got to take her first breath. "I realized I'd missed a few periods. I always got them erratically, so I didn't notice at first. Then I noticed my stomach was growing. I stole a pregnancy test and made a doctor's appointment. Bobby found the test, flipped out, and beat me so badly that I ended up in the hospital. I lost the baby, and that's when I knew. If I stayed I would die too. So I told a nurse I was in trouble."

There wasn't a single doubt in Jasmine's mind that if she hadn't left then she never would have made it out of her teens. Bobby liked his girls young. When she got too old he would have killed her and replaced her.

"You were brave, sweetheart, so very brave to do that."

Jasmine shook her head. "Didn't feel very brave. I couldn't even tell them who had hurt me because I was terrified he would take it out on my sisters. Make them do what he made me do."

Shame burned through her.

Not just because of her stupidity in believing Bobby, but in all the things she'd done to avoid a beating when she was trapped in that house. Two years locked in a small bedroom, only allowed out when she was taken to service a man who had paid Bobby for the pleasure of taking what she wasn't offering.

"I did a lot of things I wish I hadn't, Adam." If he couldn't handle that, if he thought she was dirty now he knew the truth about her, she'd rather know that now before she got any more invested.

"Oh, baby. Nothing that happened was your fault. He was an adult. You were a kid. He was a predator who preyed on young girls, luring them in and then using threats and physical violence to keep them in line. You were afraid for your life, afraid for your sisters, and if you could have saved your baby you would have. You escaped, you rebuilt your life, you built a successful business from the ground up, and you are going to be an amazing mom."

"You ... you still want me around Claire?" Jasmine was almost afraid to ask the question in case the answer was no.

Before Adam could answer, the front door to his house was thrown open and Claire came running out, Fauna at her heels.

"We waited, Daddy, but you taked too long," Claire said as she yanked open Jasmine's door and barreled into her arms.

"Careful, pumpkin, Jasmine is sore," Adam reprimanded his daughter.

"I don't mind, hugs are the best medicine," she said as she returned the little girl's hug as Fauna nosed her knee, giving it a lick.

The smile on Adam's face was everything she needed right now, and when he leaned in and touched a featherlight kiss to her cheek, she already knew what his answer was.

"The sight of you, holding my daughter, your dog watching over both of my girls, that's everything. That's our future."

A future she still wasn't sure she deserved, but one she was going to grab onto with both hands and never let go.

CHAPTER

Twenty

December 24th
8:03 P.M.

"That one's like a reindeer farm!" Claire squealed in delight.

"It's super cool," Jasmine agreed.

Adam glanced in the rear vision mirror and smiled when he saw how relaxed his girls looked. Even though Jasmine's Christmas Farm had a special Christmas Eve light show and party, they'd decided to follow his and Claire's tradition and drive around the neighborhood looking at the lights while eating popcorn and drinking hot chocolate.

"Not as cool as the reindeer on your farm," Claire qualified. "Cos theys real reindeer."

"They are and that is cool, but I think these ones are cool too. My reindeer don't change color like that," Jasmine teased as the brightly lit reindeer changed from green to yellow.

Claire giggled. "I wish real reindeer did that too."

"That would be awesome," Jasmine agreed.

Seeing her so relaxed after everything she'd been through was better than any Christmas miracle. It had been a rough week, Jasmine had had nightmares, and she'd struggled with sleeping in a bed again after sleeping in her pantry for the last year. His presence seemed to help so he'd taken to sleeping with her. Her injuries were healing, and she'd already attended an appointment with a trauma counselor that had helped her a lot too.

Most importantly, she wanted him to walk this road with her.

"You two ready to head home?" he asked. As much fun as it was, Claire was going to be difficult to settle tonight because she was a little kid and it was Christmas Eve, and Jasmine still needed a lot of rest so her body could heal.

"Well, we did finish all our hot chocolate," Jasmine said slowly, "and we're nearly out of popcorn. What do you think, munchkin? Ready to head home and get things ready for Santa's visit tonight?"

Already Jasmine was slipping so easily into co-parenting with him, and Claire had no problem respecting her as another authority figure in their home. While he was in no rush, he couldn't wait to make Jasmine his wife, and when she was ready add more children to their family.

"Do you know what Daddy and I do before I go to bed?" Claire asked, bouncing in her seat.

"Your daddy told me that you guys go outside and see if you can spot Rudolph's red nose," Jasmine replied. "It sounds like a lot of fun."

"I saw it last year, remember, Daddy?" Claire asked as she picked up a couple of pieces of popcorn from the bowl Jasmine held on her lap.

"I remember, pumpkin, it was so exciting." His eyes met Jasmine's in the rearview mirror, and they shared a smile. The innocence of youth was an amazing thing. A simple thing like the lights of a passing plane could so easily be played off as the glowing nose of a magical, flying reindeer. As much as he loved watching his daughter meet new milestones and learn new things, he was definitely going to miss her being young, sweet, and unmarred by the cold realities of the real world.

"Did the Santa's helper who works at your farm tell you what time Santa is coming?" Claire asked Jasmine.

"No, munchkin, he can't tell me things like that. That's Santa's personal business and remember he doesn't do the same country first every year, he has to make it fair to all the children in the world, and there are millions of them."

"Wow ... millions?" Claire echoed, looking intrigued.

"Yep, millions. So, Santa might not come here early tonight. We might not get to see Rudolph's glowing nose, but even if we don't we'll still have fun looking," Jasmine said.

"Yeah, so much fun," Claire quickly agreed.

Jasmine's gaze searched his out as though checking what she'd said was okay, but since Adam didn't want her thinking of herself as a second-class parent, if they were together then they were raising Claire together, he averted his gaze back to the road.

"So home it is. Then we can look for Santa's sleigh, put out our milk and cookies—"

"And carrots for the reindeer," Claire inserted.

"Right, and carrots for the reindeer. Then it's into bed for you, little pumpkin."

"Can't we watch another movie?" Claire begged even though it was already past her eight o'clock bedtime.

"Nope. We watched one with dinner," he said in his firm dad voice.

Before Claire could even think about putting in a complaint, they were driving past another house with a stunning display, this one a white mass of snowmen, and his daughter was too busy oohing and ahhing to worry about anything else.

Ten minutes later, he was pulling into his driveway. Adam had barely parked the car when Claire was wriggling and trying to get out.

"Hold on, squirmy little worm," Jasmine said as she unbuckled herself then reached over to unbuckle Claire. As soon as she was free, his daughter was scrambling out of the car.

"Over here, Jassy! This is where Daddy and I laided last year," she called out.

"Pumpkin, don't lie down till you put your coat on," he reminded his daughter as he helped Jasmine out of the car.

Grabbing all three of their coats, Adam slipped his on, then held out Jasmine's so she could slip her arms into it. Wrangling his over-excited five-year-old into her coat was a much harder task, but eventually, he zipped her up, and she immediately flopped down into the snow, lying flat on her back so she could gaze up at the sky.

"Come on, Jassy," Claire ordered, patting the ground beside her.

"I'm not sure Jasmine's up to getting down on the ground yet, pumpkin, she's still healing."

"I can do it," Jasmine said.

Doubtful but not going to stop her, instead, Adam helped Jasmine sit down on the cold, snowy ground, then stretched out on the other side of Claire, looking up at the clear sky. It had been snowing earlier and Claire had had a ball running around trying to catch snowflakes on her tongue and making snow angels, but now the snow was gone, the clouds had cleared, and it was a magical winter night.

With his two girls beside him, his daughter chattering non-stop about Santa, his sleigh, reindeer, and the glow of Rudolph's nose, and Jasmine chattering back just as excitedly he had everything in the world he'd ever wanted.

"Daddy, Jassy, look!" Claire screeched, jumping to her feet. "Red light! It's Rudolph's nose!"

The complete and utter joy on Claire's face, the peaceful and content smile on Jasmine's, both made this by far the best Christmas he'd ever had.

CHAPTER
Twenty~One

December 24th
9:18 P.M.

"Finally," Adam huffed out a sigh and leaned against the wall outside Claire's room.

They'd finally gotten a super overexcited Claire into bed and off to sleep. It had only taken about five stories to get her finally drifting off as her overtired body and mind finally gave out despite her excitement.

Jasmine couldn't wait to see the little girl's face tomorrow morning as she ran downstairs to see what Santa had left for her.

It was the first Christmas since just before her sixteenth birthday that she was actually looking forward to. Those two Christmases she'd spent as Bobby's prisoner had been pure hell, and she'd spent most of the day curled on her mattress sobbing. Then the last six she'd spent alone in her house, too ashamed to let her family back into her life.

"Now to get you into bed," he said as he scooped her up.

Her arms automatically curled around his neck. "I'm not sleepy."

"You're still recovering, you need rest. We have a big day tomorrow, lunch with my family and dinner with yours."

Lunch *and* dinner.

In the same day.

Two Christmases.

She hardly dared to believe it.

The fear that she would wake up and find this was all a dream and she was still chained to that wall in Bobby's basement was ever-present.

But she wasn't.

She was free.

Not just free from that house of horrors that had stolen two years of her life, two years that were supposed to be filled with dates, and proms, and graduation. Years she'd spent being raped by older men so Bobby Johnson could make easy money. The next six years had been lost to her too as guilt and shame had consumed her.

Now she had a whole new life to look forward to. A future she hadn't thought she deserved, but now she was beginning to accept that even though she'd been incredibly naïve to believe Bobby was who he pretended to be she hadn't committed any other sin. She'd done the best she could to protect her baby sisters the only way she knew how.

Her future was there, waiting for her to reach out and grab hold of it.

Exactly what she planned on doing.

"I'll go to bed if you come with me," she said as Adam nudged open the door to the master bedroom where she'd been sleeping since he brought her here after the hospital.

"As soon as I put the presents under the tree and in Claire's stocking, I'll join you."

"Uh uh, I want to help with that, but after, first I want you."

"You have me, green eyes."

Okay, so he was going to make her spell it out. Sex was something she was both experienced and inexperienced in. Not a virgin when she'd been forced into prostitution, she'd had a boyfriend her sophomore year and they'd slept together a few times, but nothing these last six years. She knew how to be used by a man for sex, but not what it was like for that man to know how to, or care to, make her feel good.

"I want *all* of you, Adam."

His head turned so their eyes could meet, sparks danced between them but he made no move to do anything. "You're going to have to spell it out for me, green eyes. You've been through a lot and are still recovering. I don't want to assume anything."

"You trying to embarrass me?" she grumbled.

Adam laughed. "No, sweetheart. But given your past, I need you to be clear on exactly what you want."

"You, me, in that bed, having se— making love," she amended.

A growl rumbled through his chest, and he took two long steps to get them to the bed. "Been waiting a long time to taste you, green eyes." As he laid her out on the bed and stared hungrily at her, Jasmine felt heat flush through her system.

She'd never had a man go down on her before, but as Adam reverently unzipped her jeans and slipped them down her legs, pulling off her boots and then tossing them and her jeans on the floor, she was excited to see what it was like.

"Lacy panties," he groaned as he looked at the green lace underwear she'd bought a while back when she and Adam first started dating.

"I'm wearing the matching bra," she informed him.

Another groan. "Babe, you're killing me here."

She giggled a little nervously, but when Adam took her hands and sat her up, pulling the hem of her sweater up and over her head, tossing it to join the rest of her clothes on the floor, that nervousness morphed into desire.

There was no way she could be nervous when he was staring at her with so much hunger in his deep, brown eyes.

"Lie down, green eyes," he ordered softly, and she rested back, laying her head on the pillow.

Stretching out over her, he brushed his lips across hers in a sweet kiss, a prelude to what was to come. An appetizer that already had her hungering over the main course.

"You need me to stop, Jasmine, you tell me. I won't do anything you don't like or want."

"I know that," she assured him.

When his mouth closed over one of her nipples, she gasped and arched off the bed. The wet heat through the lace of her bra felt amazing, and her nipple pebbled as he swiped the tip of his tongue across it.

Sucking on her breast one of his hands claimed her other, kneading it, tweaking the nipple between his thumb and forefinger.

Sensations buzzed through her body, filling her with feelings she'd never experienced before. Teenage sex was nothing like this. This was a whole body and mind experience, making her every nerve ending come alive, her every blood cell transporting pleasure throughout her body.

Jasmine mewed a protest when his mouth and his hand left her breasts, but then he was kissing his way down her stomach. Settling between her legs, he buried his nose in her center and dragged in a breath.

"So sweet," he murmured. "Gorgeous and sexy as they are, green eyes, they have to go."

His fingertips seemed to trail lines of fire across her skin as he slid the panties down her legs. Tossing the scrap of material aside, he buried his face between her legs again.

That first swipe of his tongue was like a little drop of heaven.

Something powerful took hold inside her.

Growing with each lick of his tongue against her core, and when his lips closed around her bud and he sucked hard it surged.

It continued to grow until it felt like almost too much, and then unable to hold it in anymore it burst like a pinata filled with treats. Only the treats were these amazing sensations that flooded through her, consuming her in a wave of pleasure that metaphorically knocked her off her feet and washed her away.

There was a somewhat smug smile on Adam's face as she blinked, and her vision cleared to find his face above hers. "Can I take it you enjoyed?"

"Oh yeah," she murmured.

"You'll always enjoy, green eyes. That's the way it should be, especially when you're in love. I love you, baby," he said as he thrust inside her, filling her in a way she hadn't even realized she was empty.

"Love you too. So much."

Setting a steady pace, Adam thrust into her, and she grabbed his shoulders, holding on as her hips rocked to meet him thrust for thrust.

His lips found hers and his kiss was full of so much love and tenderness that a second wave built inside her.

That dam burst, and more pleasure than she'd experienced in her life exploded inside her.

Love.

This was what love felt like.

Perfection.

Warmth.

Belonging.

Safety.

This place right here was where she was supposed to be.

CHAPTER
Twenty~Two

December 25th
6:20 A.M.

"Santa's been!"

The squealed words snapped him out of a deep sleep, and Adam blinked open heavy eyes to see Claire bouncing from foot to foot in the bedroom doorway.

Beside him, Jasmine also stirred. From the way she stiffened, he assumed she was wondering what his daughter's reaction would be to seeing them in bed together. Even though they'd been sleeping together for the last few nights, they both knew it was different now that they'd had sex.

Claire, on the other hand, had no idea that things had changed between him and Jasmine last night, nor did she care.

All a little girl cared about on Christmas morning was the presents waiting by the tree.

"You knew he would, pumpkin," he reminded her.

"I know, Daddy, but there's so many presents," she said, still bouncing about like she'd already eaten a pound of sugar.

"Morning, green eyes, Merry Christmas." Leaning over, he touched a kiss to Jasmine's lips and loved the way she blushed. If she was embarrassed about them kissing in front of his daughter, she better get used to it. They were a couple, and they were going to spend the rest of their lives together. Besides, Claire didn't care, she was as excited about Jasmine joining their family as he was.

"Come on, Daddy. Come on, Jassy. Hurry, hurry, hurry," Claire said as though she were about to burst.

"We're coming, pumpkin."

"Wouldn't want to make you wait a second longer than you have to," Jasmine added.

Thankful they'd thought to put pajamas on last night before they laid down to go to sleep, they pushed back the covers and climbed out of bed. Before they even reached the door, Claire had grabbed both their hands and was pulling them toward the stairs.

Together as a family, they took seats on the floor around the Christmas tree. Because Jasmine was still hurting, Adam piled up some pillows for her to sit on, and once he'd started a fire in the fireplace, and turned on the Christmas tree lights, he sat behind her, nestling her between his knees so she could lean against his chest.

"Now, Daddy?" Claire asked, her smile so wide he was surprised her cheeks weren't hurting.

"Now, pumpkin."

With all the joy of an innocent child on this magical morning, Claire giggled and squealed her excitement as she opened each of the gifts sitting under the tree and the ones from her stocking. There were candies, barrettes for her hair, makeup to play with, a couple of new dresses and a new pair of sneakers, some doll she'd been raving about for months, a pair of roller skates, and a bunch of books since Claire loved to read.

By the time her stocking was empty, the only gifts left under the tree were the ones they'd be taking to his parents' place for lunch and Jasmine's for dinner, and the gifts he and Jasmine had to exchange with one another.

"Daddy, can we give Jassy her present now?" Claire asked, still bouncing about as excited to give gifts as she was to receive them.

"You bet. Why don't you get it." Some things were just from him, but Claire had been excited about this gift for Jasmine since her birthday. Adam was kind of surprised his daughter had actually managed to keep it a secret for the last three months.

"I can't wait to see what you guys got me," Jasmine said. Her smile was wide and genuine, and there was a peace in her eyes that hadn't been there the entire time he'd known her. She might still have a long road ahead of her to recover from everything she'd been through, but knowing she was no longer traversing that road alone seemed to have made all the difference.

"Here, Jassy!" Claire was practically bursting with delight as she handed over the box.

"Ooh, penguins, I love penguins," Jasmine exclaimed as she took the box a little awkwardly with one of her arms still in a cast.

"I know. I chose-ed it just for you. You should get penguins at your farm." Claire clapped her hands in obvious joy at the idea.

"Maybe, that would be fun," Jasmine agreed as she balanced the box on her lap and pulled on one end of the bow to undo it.

As he watched her lift the lid off, Adam found he was as excited as Claire. While he still had the canvas portrait for her, this gift was from both him and his daughter, and it had been inspired by the gift Jasmine gave Claire for her birthday. They'd planned this out together, a daddy and daughter team, and when it had been made and arrived, they had spent hours looking at it. Even though it had been tucked away in the back of his closet, Claire had asked several times to get it out and look at it.

"Oh," Jasmine gasped as she looked inside the box. Tears filled her eyes as she looked up at him and Claire, but her smile was so bright it was like sunlight. "You guys, this is ... I don't even ... it's beautiful, it's amazing, it's the best gift I've ever been given."

"It's you, see." Claire scrambled up and onto Jasmine's lap, pointing out the blonde figure in the open music box. "And that's me, and that's daddy. Oh, and Fauna too."

At the sound of her name, the dog lifted her head from where she was lounging by the fire and gave a wag of her tail.

"We're at your farm. Look there's Santa's house, the reindeer, and the elves' workshop, and we're building a snowman," Claire babbled.

"All of us together," Jasmine said softly.

"Yeah, cos we's a family," Claire said like it was obvious.

"A family," Jasmine repeated.

Lifting both his girls, Adam set them in his lap. Fauna not wanting to be left out bounded over and clambered onto Claire's lap making his daughter giggle.

"We're a family now, the three of us," Adam said.

"Four, Daddy," Claire corrected. "Don't forget Fauna."

Adam laughed. "Sure, the four of us, one day we might add a baby to our family."

"A sister," Claire piped up.

"Or a brother," he reminded her, not wanting her to get hung up on a sister since there was just as much chance it might be a brother instead. "For now, though, I think our family is pretty perfect."

"Perfect," Jasmine echoed.

"Perfectly perfect," Claire added, not to be left out.

With the crackling fire, the twinkling lights, the discarded wrapping paper and gift boxes, the Christmas tree, and decorations everywhere, and his two girls on his lap, Adam couldn't think of anything that would make this moment more perfect.

Best Christmas ever by far.

Will Christmas bring happiness to Jessica and her young son Freddie? Holiday Loss coming Christmas 2024

Holiday Loss (Christmas Romantic Suspense #8)

Also by Jane Blythe

Detective Parker Bell Series

A SECRET TO THE GRAVE
WINTER WONDERLAND
DEAD OR ALIVE
LITTLE GIRL LOST
FORGOTTEN

Count to Ten Series

ONE
TWO
THREE
FOUR
FIVE
SIX
BURNING SECRETS
SEVEN
EIGHT
NINE
TEN

Broken Gems Series

CRACKED SAPPHIRE

CRUSHED RUBY

FRACTURED DIAMOND

SHATTERED AMETHYST

SPLINTERED EMERALD

SALVAGING MARIGOLD

River's End Rescues Series

COCKY SAVIOR

SOME REGRETS ARE FOREVER

SOME FEARS CAN CONTROL YOU

SOME LIES WILL HAUNT YOU

SOME QUESTIONS HAVE NO ANSWERS

SOME TRUTH CAN BE DISTORTED

SOME TRUST CAN BE REBUILT

SOME MISTAKES ARE UNFORGIVABLE

Candella Sisters' Heroes Series

LITTLE DOLLS

LITTLE HEARTS

LITTLE BALLERINA

Storybook Murders Series

NURSERY RHYME KILLER

FAIRYTALE KILLER

FABLE KILLER

Saving SEALs Series

Prey Security Series

Prey Security: Alpha Team Series

Prey Security: Artemis Team Series

IVORY'S FIGHT

PEARL'S FIGHT

LACEY'S FIGHT

OPAL'S FIGHT

Prey Security: Bravo Team Series

VICIOUS SCARS

RUTHLESS SCARS

Christmas Romantic Suspense Series

CHRISTMAS HOSTAGE

CHRISTMAS CAPTIVE

CHRISTMAS VICTIM

YULETIDE PROTECTOR

YULETIDE GUARD

YULETIDE HERO

HOLIDAY GRIEF

Conquering Fear Series (Co-written with Amanda Siegrist)

DROWNING IN YOU

OUT OF THE DARKNESS

CLOSING IN

About the Author

USA Today bestselling author Jane Blythe writes action-packed romantic suspense and military romance featuring protective heroes and heroines who are survivors. One of Jane's most popular series includes Prey Security, part of Susan Stoker's OPERATION ALPHA world! Writing in that world alongside authors such as Janie Crouch and Riley Edwards has been a blast, and she looks forward to bringing more books to this genre, both within and outside of Stoker's world. When Jane isn't binge-reading she's counting down to Christmas and adding to her 200+ teddy bear collection!

To connect and keep up to date please visit any of the following